Also by Édouard Louis

A Woman's Battles and Transformations

Who Killed My Father

History of Violence

The End of Eddy

CHANGE

CHANGE

ÉDOUARD LOUIS

Translated from the French by
John Lambert

Farrar, Straus and Giroux
New York

Farrar, Straus and Giroux
120 Broadway, New York 10271

Library of Congress Cataloging-in-Publication Data
Names: Louis, Édouard, author. | Lambert, John, 1960– translator.
Title: Change : a novel / Édouard Louis ; translated from the French by
    John Lambert.
Other titles: Changer. English
Description: First American edition. | New York : Farrar, Straus and
    Giroux, 2024.
Identifiers: LCCN 2023038960 | ISBN 9780374606800 (hardcover)
Subjects: LCSH: Louis, Édouard—Fiction. | Authors, French—Fiction. |
    Alienation (Social psychology)—France—Fiction. | Social capital
    (Sociology)—France—Fiction. | France—Fiction. | LCGFT:
    Autobiographical fiction. | Novels.
Classification: LCC PQ2712.O895 C5713 2024 | DDC 843/.92—dc23/
    eng/20231002
LC record available at https://lccn.loc.gov/2023038960

Designed by Patrice Sheridan

Our books may be purchased in bulk for promotional, educational, or business
use. Please contact your local bookseller or the Macmillan Corporate and
Premium Sales Department at 1-800-221-7945, extension 5442, or by email at
MacmillanSpecialMarkets@macmillan.com.

www.fsgbooks.com
Follow us on social media at @fsgbooks

1   3   5   7   9   10   8   6   4   2

I AM NO LONGER ANYTHING, ONLY A PRETEXT.

—Jean Genet, *The Thief's Journal*

TWO PROLOGUES

IT'S 12:33 A.M. AND I START TO WRITE IN THIS DARK AND silent room. Outside through the open window I hear voices in the night and police sirens in the distance.

I'm twenty-six years and a few months old; most people would say that my life is ahead of me, that nothing has started yet, but for a long time now I've been living with the feeling that I've lived too much; I imagine that's why the need to write is so deep, to fix the past in writing and, I suppose, to get rid of it, or maybe, conversely, the past is so anchored in me now that I'm forced to talk about it, at every moment, on every occasion, maybe it has won out, and by believing I'm getting rid of it I'm only bolstering its existence and its ascendancy over my life, maybe I'm trapped—I don't know.

When I was twenty-one it was already too late, I'd already lived too much—I'd known misery, poverty in my childhood, my mother asking me time and again to go and knock on the neighbors' or my aunt's door with an imploring voice so they'd give us a packet of pasta and a jar of tomato sauce because she had no more money and she knew that a child would be more easily pitied than an adult.

I'd known violence, my cousin who died in prison at thirty, my older brother who was sick with alcoholism even as a teenager, who woke up drunk most mornings because his body was so steeped in alcohol, my mother who denied it with all her might to protect her son who swore to us every time he drank that it was the last time, that after that he'd never drink again. The fights in the village café, the obsessive racism of rural, isolated communities, underlying every sentence, or even every word, *This isn't France anymore, it's Africa, there's nothing but foreigners everywhere you look*; the constant fear of not making it to the end of the month, not being able to buy wood to heat the house or replace the children's torn shoes, my mother's words, *I don't want my kids to be ashamed at school*; and my father, sick from a life of working in the factory, on the assembly line, then in the streets sweeping other people's rubbish, my grandfather sick from the same life, sick because his life was almost an exact replica of his great-grandfather's, his grandfather's, his father's and his son's: deprivation, precarity, quitting school at fourteen or fifteen, life in the factory, sickness. When I was six or seven I looked at these men around me and I thought that their lives would be mine, that one day I'd go to the factory like them and that the factory would break my back as well.

I'd escaped from this fate and worked in a bakery, as a caretaker, a bookseller, a waiter, an usher, a secretary, a tutor, a sex worker, a monitor in a summer camp, a guinea pig for medical experiments. Miraculously, I'd attended what's considered one of the most prestigious universities in Europe and graduated with a degree in philosophy and sociology, whereas no one else in my family had studied at all. I'd read Plato, Kant, Derrida, de Beauvoir. After growing up among the poorest classes of northern France, I'd got to know the provincial middle classes, their sourness, and then, later on, the Parisian intellectual world, the French and international upper classes. I'd rubbed shoulders with some of the richest people in the world. I'd made love to men who had works by Picasso, Monet and Soulages in their living rooms, who traveled only by private jet and spent their entire time in hotels where one night, one single night, cost what my whole family earned in a year when I was a child, for a family of seven.

I'd been close—physically at least—to the aristocracy, I'd dined at the homes of dukes and princesses, eaten caviar and drunk rare champagnes with them several times a week, spent my holidays in big houses in Switzerland with the mayor of Geneva who'd become my friend. I'd known the life of drug dealers, loved a railway maintenance worker and another man who, at barely thirty, had spent a third of his life in prison, and slept in the arms of yet another on an estate reputed to be one of the toughest in France.

At just over twenty I'd changed my first and last names in court, transformed my face, redesigned my hairline, undergone several operations, reinvented the way I moved, walked and talked, and got rid of the northern accent of my childhood. I'd fled to Barcelona to start a new life with a fallen aristocrat, tried to give up everything and move to India, lived in a tiny studio in Paris, owned a huge apartment in one of the richest neighborhoods in New York, walked for weeks alone across the United States, through unknown, ghostly cities, in an attempt to unravel what my life had become. When I went back to see my father or mother we didn't know what to say to each other, we no longer spoke the same language, everything I'd experienced in such a short time, everything I'd gone through, everything separated us.

I'd written and published books before I turned twenty-five, and traveled the world to talk about them, to Japan, Chile, Kosovo, Malaysia and Singapore. I'd been asked to speak at Harvard, Berkeley, the Sorbonne. At first this life awed me, then it left me jaded and disgusted.

I'd narrowly escaped death, I'd experienced death, felt its reality, I'd lost the use of my body for several weeks.

More than anything else I'd wanted to escape my child-hood, the gray skies of the Nord department and the doomed life of my childhood friends whom society had deprived of everything, their only prospect of happiness being the couple of evenings a week they spent at the village bus stop, drinking beer and pastis in plastic cups to forget, to forget reality. I'd dreamed of being recognized in the street, dreamed of being invisible, dreamed of disappearing, dreamed of waking up one morning as a girl, dreamed of being rich, dreamed of starting all over again.

At times I'd have liked to lie down in a corner, away from everything, to dig a hole, burrow into it and never speak again, never move again, along the lines of what Nietzsche calls Russian fatalism: like those soldiers who, exhausted from fighting, crushed by the fatigue of battle and their pained, heavy bodies, lie down on the ground, in the snow, far from the others, and wait for death to come.

It is this story—this odyssey—that I want to try to tell here.

I CLIMBED THE STAIRS TWO AT A TIME. I NO LONGER know what I was thinking about in that stairwell, I imagine I was counting the steps so as not to think of anything else.

I arrived at the door, caught my breath and rang the bell. The man approached from the other side, I could hear him, I could make out his footsteps on the wooden floor.

I'd met him on the Internet just two hours earlier. He was the one who'd contacted me. He'd told me he liked boys like me, young, slender, blond, blue-eyed—the Aryan type, he'd insisted. He'd asked me to dress like a student and that's what I'd done—at least his idea of a student—with an oversized hoodie I'd borrowed from Geoffroy and sky-blue trainers, my favorites, I'd done what he wanted because I was hoping he'd reward my efforts and pay me more than he'd promised.

I waited.

Finally, he opened the door and at the sight of him I had to tense my face to keep from grimacing—he didn't look like the photos he'd sent, his body was flabby, heavy, I don't know how to put it, as if he was sagging or rather oozing to the floor.

Just coming to the door had been a strain for him, I could see his fatigue, his shortness of breath, the dozens of tiny drops of sweat shining on his forehead. I tried to look at him as little as possible, I wanted to avoid seeing the details of his face. In less than an hour you'll be out of here with the money, I thought. His odor reached me, a synthetic smell of vanilla and sour milk. I focused on that sentence—In less than an hour, the money—when suddenly I heard voices behind him in the flat. They belonged to men, several of them, maybe three or four. I asked who they were, he smiled and said: It's nothing. Pretend they're not here, they're used to it, I often bring in whores, you're not the first. You ignore them and we'll go to my room.

I thought: I don't want other people seeing my face—the shame began to rise inside me, from the tips of my fingers to the nape of my neck, like a warm, paralyzing fluid, I recognized its burn. I threatened to go home. I thought it would hurt or irritate him but he didn't try to stop me. Calmly he offered to give me fifty euros for the trip if I wanted to turn and go, and I hated him for not getting angry. I needed more than fifty euros. Okay, I said, we'll go straight to your room, they won't see me, I'll pull up my hood.

He promised me his friends wouldn't try to see my face, they don't give a shit; he was already turning around, I could see his fat white neck. Think of the money, think of the money.

I crossed the living room with him. He walked in front of me. I lowered my head, the hood hiding my face. In the bedroom he sat on the edge of his bed, the weight of his heavy body on the mattress produced a high-pitched creaking sound.

The mattress screamed in my place.

I stood there, facing his body, I didn't dare move, he looked at me Fuck you're a turn-on with your little Nazi face. I didn't say anything, I knew my silence would please him, that was what he wanted and what he was paying me for, my toughness, my coldness. I was playing a role. He asked me to undress, he said: As slowly as possible, and I did.

Now I was naked in front of him, waiting. He just said: I want you to fuck me like a slut. He straightened up, pulled his trousers down to his knees, without taking them off completely, turned and got on all fours on the bed—his ass in front of me too white and too red, flaccid, limp, covered with little brown hairs. Go on, fuck me, fuck me like I'm your little slut, he repeated. I rubbed my cock against his body but nothing happened, my cock remained inert, I failed, I wasn't able to think of anything else, to imagine myself in another situation, the reality of his body won out, as if it was so brutal, so total, that it made any attempt at imagination impossible. Can't do it? he asked and to buy time I said Shut the fuck up. I felt his body shudder under my fingers, he loved it.

I tried again, rubbed against him, on him, desperately, forcing myself to imagine another body in place of his body, another body under my body, or rather on my body, because I knew that was what usually turned me on. I concentrated, but the contact with his dry, cold skin brought me back to the truth and his presence. He started to sigh to show his impatience. I told you shut the fuck up and don't move, I repeated, but I knew it wouldn't work as well the second time. He wanted something else. I rubbed myself even harder against him but I knew I'd already lost, I'd lost from the start, today I look back and I think I knew that the moment I entered his room.

I thought of the money I needed, the shame the next day if I had to tell the dentist I couldn't pay him, the look in his eyes and the words he must have known by heart, Can I pay you next time, I'm sorry, I don't have my wallet, I forgot it, he'd have known I was lying and I'd have known he knew, and I thought of the shame this infinite game of mirrors would cause—it was as simple, as banal as that, that was why I was in this man's house, naked against him.

He was still in the same position, motionless on all fours. I backed up a bit, walked around the bed and came to stand in front of him. His features were drawn, his face was pleading, exhausted from waiting. Suck, I said, and he took my still soft cock in his mouth. I closed my eyes. I don't know how I managed, but after about twenty minutes standing there in front of him my cock bulged and I came, I pulled out of his mouth to cover his face, and looking down I saw the thick, white liquid on his forehead, his cheeks, his eyelids.

My breath shook.

I got dressed. I thought: It's almost over. Almost over. He grabbed a towel from the bedside table that he'd probably put there knowing I'd come, wiped his face and walked over to a small chest of drawers. He took out a wad of notes and came over to me.

He gave me a hundred euros; I didn't move. He knew exactly what I was expecting and why I didn't move but he pretended not to understand. He was playing with me, he knew full well that I saw what was going on, that I knew he was playing with me but that I was too afraid to say anything. Finally he said You did half the job so I'm paying you half the money. You should have fucked me, you didn't. A whore who doesn't fuck isn't a whore. You can be glad I'm giving you a hundred. He didn't say it aggressively but more as an observation, the way you cite a rule or the terms of a contract. I'd learned to recognize how rich someone was at a glance, I could see it, I was never wrong, I knew he was rich and that paying me a hundred euros more wouldn't have changed a thing for him, that having a hundred euros less in his wallet wouldn't have made the slightest impact on his life. My heart was pounding in my chest (it wasn't my heart that was pounding but my whole body). I started to describe my situation to this man in front of me, I didn't even know his name but I told him everything, the shame, the dentist. That wasn't his problem, he said, when you do things by halves you get half what you bargained for. You have to know what you want in life. You're young, you have time to learn.

It was when he said those words that I decided to back down. His friends in the next room could get worried and come in to see if everything was all right, they couldn't see my face—They mustn't see your face, Other people must not see your face.

———

I took the money and left, walked through Paris in the night, and went home. Outside, the pavements were shiny from the rain, reflecting the streets like a second city projected onto the ground. I walked. I didn't think I hated him. I didn't think anything.

When I entered my flat I sat on the edge of the bed and cried. Even when I was crying I didn't think anything. I no longer knew my name. I wasn't crying because of what had just happened, which wasn't such a big deal, just the sort of unpleasant thing that can happen to you in any situation; rather, what had just happened allowed me to cry for all the times in my life when I hadn't cried, all the times I'd held back. It's possible during that night, in that room, I let my eyes cry twenty years of uncried tears.

I walked to the shower. I didn't take off my clothes. I turned on the warm water and felt it run down over me, from the top of my head to my ankles. I tilted my head back, stretching my throat, and opened my mouth as if I was going to scream, a long, beautiful scream, but I didn't. The water soaked my clothes, my white T-shirt turned the color of my skin, my soggy trousers grew dark and heavy.

I stayed under that shower for a long time, watching the water running down over me. When I got out morning was breaking. I think it was then that I asked myself if one day I'd be able to write a scene like that, a scene so far removed from the child I'd been and his world, not a tragic or pathetic scene but above all one that was radically foreign to that child, and it was then that I promised myself I'd do it one day, that one day I'd tell everything that had led up to that scene and everything that happened afterward, as a way of going back in time.

I

ELENA

(fictional conversations with my father)

NEED I TELL YOU AGAIN HOW IT ALL STARTED? I GREW UP in a world that rejected everything I was, and I experienced that as an injustice because—as I repeated to myself a hundred times a day, to the point of nausea—I didn't choose what I was.

I've said all this before but I have to put it in order, I promised it to myself, the problem was diagnosed in the first years of my life: when I learned to speak, when I started to express myself, to move in the world, I heard more and more people around me asking Why does Eddy speak like that, why does he talk like a girl when he's a boy? Why does he walk like a girl? Why does he twist his hands when he speaks? Why does he look at other boys like that? Could it be that he's a bit queer?

I didn't choose to walk the way I did, to talk the way I did, I didn't understand why I had those mannerisms—that's what the people in the village called them, Eddy's mannerisms,

Eddy has mannerisms when he talks—I didn't understand why those mannerisms had been imposed on me, on my body. I don't know why I was attracted to other boys' bodies and not to girls' bodies as would have been expected of me. I was a prisoner of myself. At night I dreamed of changing, of becoming someone else, and it was perhaps in those early years of my life that the idea of change became so central for me.

You were one of the first to worry. At night, when you were with Mom in your bedroom, I could hear you two talking—there were no doors between the rooms, buying doors would have cost too much money, and you'd hung up curtains you'd found at the junk shop. I could smell the cigarettes you smoked one after the next in your bed, the smoke and above all your voices reached me in the darkness, Why does Eddy talk like that? We didn't bring him up to be a queer, I don't get it. Can't he act a bit normal?

Queer. At five or six I understood that this word would define me and that it would stick with me for the rest of my life.

What you don't know, because I hid it from you, is that it followed me everywhere, not just at home but also in the streets of the village, at school, everywhere, and that you weren't the only one who worried.

(Or did you know that and just not say anything to protect yourself from the truth?)

What you also don't know is that the insults made everything else unbearable for me, our poverty, our way of life, the constant racism in the village, as if exclusion forced me to invent my own value system—one in which I had a place.

When Mom told us in the evening that we had no money and nothing to eat, the insults made the hunger even worse. When we no longer had any wood to heat the house, I suffered far worse from the cold than the others because of the insults. When I heard the women at the bakery or in the town square saying There're too many foreigners in France, nothing but Blacks everywhere you look, I despised them and spontaneously felt on the side of those they wanted to oppress and eradicate.

I don't know how it's possible to have such precise and somehow also adult and anachronistic thoughts as a child, but I remember that I wanted to leave the village and become rich, powerful and famous because I thought the power I'd gain through wealth and fame would be my revenge against you and the world that had rejected me. I'd be able to look at you and everyone else I'd known in the first part of my life, and say Look where I am now. You insulted me but today I'm more powerful than you, you were wrong to despise me and call me weak and now you're going to pay for your mistakes. You're going to pay for not loving me.

I wanted to succeed* out of revenge.

Deep down, what did you know? What didn't you know, what did you choose to ignore? Did you guess what I was going through? Did you wonder?

---

* This word, *succeed*, seems stupid to me now but it didn't at the time, it was what gave me the strength to escape.

I never told you that when the students had to form teams in PE at school, most often to play football or handball, I was never chosen, no one wanted me on their team. (I'm not sad telling you this today, I don't want you to feel sorry for me, I just want you to know—*to go back in time*.)

Such scenes of childhood suffering are among the most banal and predictable that there are, we've all seen them a thousand times in books and films, and yet they were among the ones that hurt me the most.

It was always the same: two pupils were chosen to form opposing teams. The gymnasium smelled of plastic, the shiny floors gave off a violent and sickening odor that mingled with the smell of sweat. The two who'd been chosen to form the teams, almost always two boys, took turns saying a name, and when someone's name was called they had to line up behind the one who'd called it.

The group with everyone who hadn't been chosen got smaller and smaller, the bodies around me disappeared. In the end, when I was the only one left, when my name was the only name that hadn't been called, one of the two captains shrugged and sighed, "Okay then, Eddy," and I could feel the others' disappointment at having me on their team, I could feel all their eyes on me.

It wasn't not being chosen that hurt, but being seen by the others as the one who hadn't been chosen. Often when I joined the group that had been forced to take me someone would whisper, "Homo on board we're toast." The adult who was supervising our class would pretend not to have heard.

That scene was repeated detail for detail, almost without variation, several dozen times during my childhood.

The same tone of voice, the same disappointment when it came time to say my name.

Another thing I didn't tell you is why I refused to go skiing with the rest of my class. Every year the school organized a week's skiing for students in year 8, practically for nothing, just fifty euros or so, and even that could be covered by social security. Hardly a family in the region could afford a ski trip, for most of the kids it was the only time in their lives they'd go on holiday, the only chance they'd get to leave the damp cold of northern France for a few days.

I told you I didn't want to go. You insisted. I said no again, I stuck to my guns. No one understood. I lied, I said I didn't feel like it and that I wasn't interested in skiing and you got angry, you said I had no idea, I couldn't say I didn't like it because I'd never tried it.

I didn't tell you that it was because I knew the ski resort had group dorms and if I went I'd be sleeping for several days in the same room as the other guys in my class, the ones who called me a fairy in the playground, slapped me when they passed me in the corridor between classes, for nothing, just for fun, who put notes in my satchel with the words "Die faggot," and who sighed in dismay when they had to have me on their team in PE.

I never told you that I didn't want to go skiing because I was afraid. Because those boys scared me. I never told you that of course like any child I dreamed of seeing the snow and the mountains.

What I didn't yet know was that the insults and the fear would save me from you, from the village, from replicating your life. I didn't yet know that humiliation would force me to be free.

MY CHILDHOOD HOME

THIS TOO I DIDN'T TELL YOU, YOU OR ANYONE ELSE: when I realized that my only option was to escape, I looked for every possible way out.* Not a day went by when I didn't think, I have to go, I have to go—this sentence became part and parcel of what I was.

One of my first real attempts to escape was when an actor came to the village to present a TV show—do you remember?

That was unheard of, no one ever came to our village in this cold, gray region, twenty kilometers from the nearest town. When I saw the poster announcing his visit I took a sheet of paper and wrote My name is Eddy Bellegueule, I want to become an actor, I want to leave this village, I'll do anything you want, contact me. I reread it and added my phone number in the bottom right corner. I was twelve. All day long I waited

---

* In my first book I explained how I did everything I could not to run away, not to be different. Both stories are true, they simply tell two sides of the same phenomenon, the same life.

in the car park of the community center next to the old metal factory, where, someone had told me, the actor would arrive and his car would be parked.

I waited there for hours, sitting on the gravel with the sun on my forearms and the dry white dust of the gravel between my fingers. Finally the car appeared; I straightened up and watched the people get out, the actor and two or three others, assistants no doubt; they had the bodies of another life, privileged, comfortable. I let them walk away and then I went up to the car and jammed my little letter between the windscreen and the wiper blade. I went home, walked past you without saying a word, lay down on my bed and hoped for weeks for an answer that never came.

I made other attempts, other efforts to tear myself away from my hated childhood, but when liberation came it was through school, that little building made of red bricks and corrugated metal that you had attended before me, the Collège des Cygnes, where all the children of the families from our region went (or not quite all of them, the richest went to private schools in the city).

There I tried everything, I joined every club and association, the chess club, the calligraphy workshop, the comic-book club, even though I hated comic books.

I devoted all my energy and time to these clubs so I wouldn't be alone at break time or lunch, but also and above all because of a vague feeling that in one of these workshops I might find a vocation or discover a talent that would allow me to leave, live another life, become rich and powerful and get my revenge.

It was through the theater that I escaped. You know that.

You felt right away that the theater would separate us; when I came home from rehearsals you'd get pissed off, Can't you stop this theater bullshit? One of the French teachers had started a club that met once a week in the late afternoon in the gray oval room beside the library.

I got to the first session before everyone else. The teacher, Aude Detrez, had us act out little scenes she'd written herself, and it was there in that room, in front of her, that the surprise happened.

The fact is that acting came astonishingly easy to me. I think it was because I knew how to play a role. I'd learned to do it in spite of myself since my early childhood; I'd played roles to try to hide who I was, to protect myself. From my youngest days I'd tried to hide my desire for other boys, I'd done my best to be more masculine, to fit in with the most hackneyed images of masculinity, to memorize the names of football players, to drink beer at the village bus stop with the other boys until late at night, to pretend I was interested in girls, I'd done all of that to put a stop to the beatings and insults at school, and limit the presence of insults in my life as much as I could.

My whole life I'd tried to pretend I was someone I wasn't, and because of all that, thanks to all that, acting was natural for me, not as an artistic vocation but simply as the continuation of my life.

I walked over to the little platform under the whiteboard, acted out the skit printed on the sheet of paper I was holding in my hand. I wasn't afraid, and I saw the eyes of the other students widen, their surprise, their admiration as I spoke and acted. I'd never felt admired before. When I finished they all applauded, shouting, Bravo, bravo, there in that little room, and it was as if all of a sudden the sound of their applause drowned out the sound of all the insults I'd heard in the past years, the insults I'd learned even as I learned to say my name. Wow, what talent, the teacher said—and I know it's naive to say but I have to because it's how I felt at that moment: when she congratulated me on my talent I felt loved. And I knew, I grasped that maybe this was how I could escape.

From that day on I clung to the theater with all my might. I wanted it to save me from poverty, from violence, from the village. The head teacher, Madame Coquet, told me that in Amiens, the big city located thirty or so kilometers away, there was a lycée with an artistic program offering theater classes, and that I should try out for it. I practiced for months, Madame Coquet's daughter helped me, she rehearsed the scenes with me: Listen to me, Nawal, I don't have much time, I repeated in the evenings, hundreds of times, and then I had the audition at the lycée and was accepted. I was the first one in our family to go to a lycée, which was a barrier that almost no one in the village overcame. I understood that the lycée symbolized the beginning of our separation, with no going back.

THE FIRST DAYS AT THE LYCÉE WERE THE FIRST DAYS OF my life away from you. I try to remember. That was where it came home to me that there were much deeper and more complex kinds of separation than geographical distance. Now I know that if I'd put thousands of kilometers between us and gone to live in a village on the other side of the world, on another continent, I wouldn't have been as far from you as I was when I walked through the doors of this school, barely thirty kilometers from where you were born.

First of all, there was the city. You never wanted to go there. You said big cities were dangerous because of the foreigners—the word you used to talk about Black people and Arabs, everyone who didn't have white skin—and that's why you refused to go there even though it wasn't so far away. Apart from the odd trip to the supermarket, we stayed in the village.

I'd grown up with you in the countryside almost never having left it, and when I arrived in Amiens at fourteen I saw a city for the first time. I imagine that if I'd been close to you,

if we'd had a relationship like the fathers and sons we saw in
films and TV series, I'd have told you when I came back home
for the weekend how fascinated I was by everything I was
discovering, the traffic, the lights that allowed people to cross
the street on foot, how you could go into shops as if it was the
easiest and most natural thing in the world, whereas for me
going into a shop had always been an event, how amazed I
was—but I didn't say a thing.

Above all I realized that I wasn't like the others at school.
They hadn't grown up in the same world as us, and through
them I learned, not that I belonged to a class, because deep
down I'd always been aware of that, but rather what that
meant in concrete terms. They talked in the corridors about
plays and films and swapped stories about where they'd gone
on their holidays. I'd never traveled abroad, I'd never been to
the theater or the cinema, no one in the village had been to the
cinema apart from the screenings put on at the community
center three times a year.

Looking at them I suddenly realized that my mother
hadn't studied, that she slurred her words when she spoke,
that in the fourteen years we'd lived together I'd never seen
her with a book in her hands. I learned that it wasn't normal
for a whole family to wash in the same bath to save water,
as we'd done when I was a child—the last person washed in
mud-colored water—that no one at the lycée had ever done
things like that. Not being able to eat every night and having to go ask my aunt or the neighbor for food wasn't normal either, that wasn't *life*, as I'd thought, but *a life*, and the
people around me in Amiens had had another life, a gentler,

more privileged one. I understood that having watched TV for seven or eight hours a day for my whole childhood meant that I was from a particular background, the world of the underprivileged, the poor—what the rich see from the outside as the world of lost childhoods. For them, I learned, studying was as natural as not studying was for us. It was only once I got to Amiens that I saw all this. I had to get away from the past to understand it, and if I wanted to write a chronological autobiography I'd have to start with Amiens and only then tell the story of the village, because I had to get to the lycée to really *see* my childhood.

Everything, every detail, separated me from the others, even the clothes; they wore jeans, polo shirts, sweaters and coats, I wore tracksuit bottoms and hoodies because that's what they wore in the village: like what the rap singers wore on TV, it looked masculine, manly. At the lycée none of that meant anything anymore.

THE MEETING WITH ELENA. SHE WAS THE ONE WHO would bring about the definitive break with you and the world we'd shared.

I was with Romain when I first saw her. It's strange, I'd arrived at the lycée thinking I'd start a new life, and the first thing I did was to define myself in relation to the expectations of my past. In the village and at school I'd always been friends with girls, Amélie, Blanche, Coralie. I'd never really managed to make friends with other boys even though I sometimes spent time with them, and I understood that you were ashamed of me when I overheard you talking with Mom, I've never forgotten what you said or how you said it: Why doesn't he play football with the other boys? Why does he always play with girls? It's not normal at his age, he should be friends with boys. I'd suffered from this inability, and I thought I'd be able to make up for it in Amiens. Simply put, I thought when I showed up in a place where I knew no one and no one knew me I'd be able to reinvent myself; I thought if I controlled my body, my mannerisms, my voice (I practiced speaking with a deeper voice), no one at the school could call me a queer, arriving at the lycée could be the start of a new life and the end of insults, and I could be friends with other boys—in the village I had the feeling the boys stayed away from me because of my reputation, and in a place where I had no reputation, no past and therefore no history, I could start over.

I'd been sitting next to Romain almost by accident one day during a French class and he spoke to me. In him I saw a chance to make up for the lost years; I thought, I'm finally going to be friends with a boy, and I swear the idea made me tremble with enthusiasm. I struggled and I succeeded, I became his friend. He was tall, muscular, athletic, he talked about girls—he was everything I'd failed to become. When I spoke to him I was careful to keep my voice as low as possible, not to gesticulate too much, to be more masculine. I tried hard to be interested in what he said about girls or sports and I pulled it off, you should have seen me, the illusion worked, and it was my struggle to be liked by him, my efforts and my persistence, that resulted in that scene where he showed me Elena; she was reading, sitting on the pavement with her back to the climbing tower between the cafeteria and the library, her head bent forward and her black hair hiding the upper part of her face. Romain said to me You see that girl over there? Everyone says she's nuts. The other day I went up to talk to her and she answered in Latin! In Latin!

How could I imagine that one of the biggest upheavals in my life would start with such banal words?

He dared me to go up to Elena and tell her I wanted to sleep with her. I looked at Elena, then at him, I hesitated. I was afraid to do what he was asking but I didn't want to miss an opportunity to impress him. Okay, I said, fine.

I walked over to Elena. I could feel Romain and Steve— the other guy who was with us—watching me, their laughter, and as I approached her I racked my brain for a formula, something I could say. I didn't know how to do it. I realized that persecuting others requires a certain technique, and I didn't possess it. I took a different tack: So what are you reading. She looked at me. She was suspicious, but she showed me the cover of her book, *Journey to the End of the Night*, and to save time—I could feel Steve and Romain coming nearer— I said Who's she, never heard of her. She laughed. He's a man. Céline is his last name, Louis-Ferdinand Céline—and to hide the shame that was rising in me I said the first thing that came to mind, I don't give a shit about literature anyway.

I clenched my fists in my pockets.

Now Romain and Steve were right behind us. They forced themselves to laugh as they waited for something to happen, but they were starting to get tired of it, I had to speed things up. I took a long breath, Actually I came to tell you I want to fuck you—such a stupid, vulgar thing to say. I turned to Romain and Steve. They were laughing. Elena looked at them, then at me. She told me I was immature, got up and walked away. I pretended to laugh but at that moment I felt something I'd never felt before; all of reality was morphing around me; I didn't immediately understand why or how but I felt it, I no longer wanted to laugh with Romain and Steve, it was too late, I no longer wanted to be with them; just three minutes earlier I'd have given anything to make them laugh but now that was over, I'd have liked to shout Elena's name, to run after her and ask her to come back, to tell her I was sorry, that it wasn't my fault, to explain to her that I'd just wanted them to like me but I'd made a mistake, what I wanted was for *her* to like me.

IT WAS ONE AFTERNOON IN THE LIBRARY THAT I SAW her again. I'd been spending my time there since I'd stopped talking to Romain.

I was looking something up on the Internet, I forget what, when Elena appeared. I turned off the screen and walked over to her. She sighed, If you've come back to make another one of your stupid jokes you can get lost—but I didn't let her finish. I told her I was sorry.

She sighed a second time but didn't object to me sitting next to her. I didn't say anything else. I took a book from a shelf and pretended to read, not understanding how she could stay so focused on what she was reading.

I saw her more and more often after that. She wasn't in the same class as me, but I'd meet her at lunch break or in the evening after school. It was during these moments with her that I understood how different she was. She had read hundreds of books, I'd read none. She'd seen Berlin, London, I'd never traveled. When she came to school on Monday she'd tell me that she'd been to a classical music concert with her mother at the Maison du Théâtre or the Maison de la Culture over the weekend, and I was completely out of my depth, I'd never heard of any of the composers or works she named.

What was happening was I wanted to be like Elena, right away. I wanted to have her life and participate in this universe I was discovering through her, not because I was more sensitive to art, more intelligent or more destined for that life than anyone else, but because I'd got a glimpse of an existence in which I could have a place. I'd failed to be the son you wanted, I'd failed to meet people's expectations in the village, I'd failed with Romain, I was failing everywhere and I had to find a type of existence in which a body and a story like mine would be possible, that's all.

There are truths that strike us abruptly, like desire, and others that we acquire over time. With Elena, every day I came to appreciate and understand a little more the person I was, and what I'd perceived when I arrived at the school was confirmed: I hadn't had a childhood, but a class childhood. All of my tastes, all of my practices, everything I did, everything I said, my opinions, it was all marked by the past. Your presence and the presence of our family was everywhere inside me. Where should I start? Above all it was during meals that I felt the difference and the shame. When I ate lunch with

Elena I compared what she ate to what I ate, and it was as if this gap between us symbolized all of the gaps between her life and mine. I ate fat-laden sandwiches and cheap crackers. She ate salads, fruit and pastries from the fashionable bakeries in town. Sometimes she'd look at what I was eating with distaste and say You shouldn't eat stuff like that, you'll ruin your body.

What were you doing, the day she first invited me to visit her at her home? I mean, how different were our lives on that day? She told me that her parents weren't there, they were both at work. I followed Elena and when she opened the door I understood who she was, or rather why she was the person she was; there were thousands of books, an antique piano, reproductions of paintings on the walls. The floors were carpeted, the house was full of armchairs, like invitations to read and reflect, as if Elena herself was a creation of her house's architecture; what's more her body had transformed since she'd entered, it had become a function of the house, an extension of the books and artworks that surrounded her, as if they were what determined her movements and intonations. She offered me a cup of tea, and even such a banal, anecdotal proposal transported me to another world—at home Mom would have offered a Coke or a glass of water with fruit syrup, maybe a beer or a glass of pastis, but not tea. She gave me tea and showed me the bookcases around us, the ones reserved for her father's books, the ones for her mother's. For the first time I read the names Proust, Kundera, Marx, Arendt. When Elena

saw me looking insistently at the piano, she explained that it
was her sister's, that her parents would have liked her to play
too but that she'd never had any talent for music. She laughed.

Later her mother arrived. She asked who I was and Elena
told her that I was her friend. Her answer, the word friend,
moved me. Her mother asked me questions, she told me her
name was Nadya, and before I left, as she was telling me about
the exhibitions she'd seen recently in museums in Paris, she
asked if I knew the painter Modigliani. I said no, of course
I didn't, and she gave me a pamphlet on the painters of the
mid-twentieth century, Picasso, Modigliani, Soutine. When
I left the house with the pamphlet in my hand I felt transformed. I thought: This is the life I want to live.

I'D LIKE TO REPHRASE WHAT I JUST SAID: WHEN I MET Elena I became attached to a new way of life, to the codes of a new social class, and to everything associated with this class, art, literature, the cinema, because all of that allowed me to take revenge on my childhood, to give me power over you, over my past, over poverty, over the insults, and in imitating this life I was gaining access to a world that had always intimidated you and that you had always implicitly recognized as superior (weren't you intimidated when you heard the doctor and teacher speaking their refined language?). I'd never met anyone so different from us—so socially distant—and perhaps that's what I saw in Elena, from the moment I saw her beside the climbing tower: the possibility of total and absolute escape.

I felt that in appropriating her life I was putting myself above you. When I left her house with the pamphlet on twentieth-century painters, I thought to myself that you had never known those painters existed, that you never would know, and so I possessed something you did not, and this new possession made me superior to you and to my whole family, and avenged me for all the times I'd been humiliated (*I'm sorry I thought like that but I had no choice, I needed arrogance and violence to rid myself of the past*).

Elena had become a factor of time; her presence accelerated it, her absence slowed it down—isn't that the very definition of love and friendship? In the evening I'd put off going back to the dorm to go walking with her near the cathedral or on the banks of the Somme. I'd walk, she'd talk, everything she said transformed me. I absorbed her words, I wanted to retain everything, appropriate everything, because every word she said was another word she put between you and me, between my past and me. She had opinions and ways of seeing the world I couldn't even have suspected, questions about the traditional couple, thoughts about the conflict in Palestine— I didn't even know such a place existed—pessimistic theories about being and existence inspired by the writers she read, Cendrars, Cioran, Keats. I no longer remember if I suffered from this gap between her and me, between what she knew and what I didn't, or if it gave me strength, precisely because it—and my being aware of it—confirmed that I was in another world.

What I do know is that I was increasingly aware that I wanted to change, I wanted to be like her, to know as much as she did, to be on her level and able to respond in conversations, and inevitably my first attempts were ridiculous. One afternoon in the corridor I heard a girl talking about the composer Richard Wagner. It was the first time I'd heard the name, but I saw just how refined she felt when she said "Richard Wagner." That evening in the dorm I logged on to one of the computers in the IT room and did a search on Richard Wagner. Frantically I wrote down everything I could on a piece of paper, hunched over the desk with a wild look in my eyes, and a few hours later before going to sleep I tried to memorize the notes that were still fresh in my mind. The next day between classes I said to the first guy who walked by me: "Do you know Richard Wagner? He's an amazing composer, I love his *Tristan and Isolde*." I was bluffing. He looked at me in surprise: Who cares?

I tried to read the same books as Elena to be like her, I imitated her bearing in class, her tortured handwriting, I sat with her on our monthly trips to the theater, I tagged along to retrospectives at the city's arthouse cinema (I learned about those too, the arthouse cinemas, and repeated the term endlessly in my head because its syllables seemed to condense the physiognomy of my new life—I'd walk beside Elena and think, *I'm going to an arthouse cinema*, I'm going to see an *arthouse film*).

I had a sense that literature, the theater and cinema were the tools that would lead me to a new life.

ALICE WALKER ONCE WROTE, "WHEN I LEFT MY HOME-town in Georgia at 17 and went off to college it was virtually the end of my always tenuous relationship with my father. This brilliant man, great at mathematics, unbeatable at story-telling, but unschooled beyond the primary grades, found the manners of his suddenly middle-class (by virtue of being at a college) daughter a barrier to easy contact, if not actually frightening. I found it painful to expose my thoughts in language that to him obscured more than it revealed. This separation, which neither of us wanted, is what poverty engenders. It is what injustice means."

I also remember how quickly my meeting Elena separated me from everyone who'd been part of my life before I left for Amiens. Not just you. When I came home for the weekend I no longer recognized myself in the reality that surrounded me; all it had taken was a few hours with Elena for everything I'd learned between the ages of zero and fourteen to fall to pieces. All of a sudden I could no longer stand the things I'd loved and shared with Mom and you, despite all that separated us, before I went to the lycée: the hours in front of the TV every evening, seven, eight hours before going to bed, or the days we spent playing games consoles, the wisecracks about women you used to make when your "buddies" came over for a glass of pastis, those jokes that Elena found vulgar and violent, the afternoons when there was a flea market or country fair in the village square—the few things I'd adored and that had still brought us together now became impossible.

I was angry at you because I couldn't tell you about how I'd felt when I entered Elena's house for the first time, the world that was opening up to me, the continent I was discovering through her. I'd have liked to tell someone about it, I think, and describe the violence of what was happening in my body, not a destructive violence, no, not at all, the beautiful violence of being torn away, of having a chance at freedom. I can't find the words, I don't know how to say it, before meeting Elena I knew that there were lives other than ours of course, rich and poor, privileged and marginalized, people in the village like the pharmacist and the mayor who had advantages that you didn't have, who had money and nice houses and whom we envied, but you have to enter those worlds to feel how real, how omnipresent the difference is, not only in terms of money but in the ways of thinking, walking, breathing, everything. I'd have liked to tell someone about this gulf and my fascination with it, the fact that I understood our world through Elena's and Elena's through ours (but perhaps when I say "I'd have liked to tell you this" it's only because it's too late now and because, protected by the sheer chronological impossibility, I can credit myself with the most beautiful, poetic intentions; perhaps deep down I was happy to keep these discoveries to myself, and happy with this new silence between us).

At home I'd become a stranger. Mom and you noticed this change in how I acted. I imitated what I'd seen in Amiens, I no longer said that I wanted to eat but that I wanted to have supper, I no longer wanted to watch TV in the evenings. I could no longer stand the stock phrases "they should bring back the death penalty" or "the right, the left, same difference," and it got on my nerves to hear you repeat them. "What rubbish," I sighed under my breath. I was upset that I didn't have parents like Elena's who questioned all of the assumptions underlying what they said, and I'm ashamed of having thought it because I know it's wrong, but deep down I resented you for being neither intelligent nor complex like Elena's parents. It's as if at Elena's home I discovered emotions I'd never known in my childhood, not because I'd been too young, but because I hadn't even known they existed: melancholy, artistic exaltation, torpor, and maybe it's partly true, maybe some emotions are inventions of the upper classes (this was before I realized that these classes are often incapable of certain emotions too, like anger or compassion). I'd tell Mom how she should be bringing up my little brother and sister, He shouldn't watch so much television, why don't you get them to listen to classical music, and she'd get angry. I used new words, words that were unimportant but seemed distinguished: tedious, extraordinary, bucolic, I no longer said it's late afternoon but it's teatime, words from another world, and Mom laughed at me, "If it isn't Monsieur Chic."

I wrote messages to Elena saying that I hated my mother, that I hated you both. You couldn't understand what I was becoming, I complained, you couldn't understand because no one in this family had studied or experienced what I was going through, but it wasn't true, all my lamenting was two-faced, deep down I was flattered by this incomprehension and distance.

One evening after dinner I said to Mom, I'm going to enjoy a cup of tea would you like some?—I didn't say drink tea but enjoy tea, the way Elena did. I did it to show the new person I thought I was. Mom looked at me and laughed, Oh, now he's playing Monsieur La-di-da, he's a nobleman now, now he ENJOYS tea. She pretended to laugh but I could hear how hurt she was and see it in her face.

As for you, you didn't say a thing. As always you were watching television in silence, and I have no idea what you thought of my transformation.

AFTER MY FIRST VISIT TO ELENA'S PLACE I WENT THERE increasingly often. Her mother invited me to eat with her and the girls on weekends and sleep over in the guest room next to Elena's bedroom on the top floor, and I did everything I could to go back to the village as little as possible, to distance myself even more radically from Mom and you. I wanted to hear Elena talk, to be at her house, to listen to the Glenn Gould and Keith Jarrett records she loved, or the Brahms records her mother admired. Everything else seemed like a waste of time to me. Even on weekday evenings I stayed away from the dorm where I should normally have slept; Nadya told me that her house was my house and that I could stay there as much as I liked.* Elena's little sister would play sonatas for us on the

---

* I won't talk any more about life in the dorm because I have nothing to say about it, all I have are a few dark and blurry memories, the strong smell of boiled vegetables in the dining hall in the evening, the boredom, the clothes stolen from the showers, my hidden desire for Karim the dormitory guard—I have nothing more to say, I have fewer memories than sensations.

piano while we ate, Nadya gave her daughters books, Federico García Lorca, Victor Hugo, Sylvia Plath.

Above all, everything I'd learned from you was the other way around at Elena's; her world was our world in reverse. You'd taught me that we had to watch television when we ate, that mealtimes were when we watched TV as a family, the news and then a film or a series. If Mom tried to talk or if I wanted to tell you about something that had happened at school that day you'd get angry and tell us to be quiet. You said watching TV in the evening was the polite thing to do. We had four or five TV sets at home, one in each bedroom, one in the living room, you'd get them from the dump and repair them. We watched TV in the morning before going to school, in the evening before going to sleep, in the afternoon on weekends. At Elena's there were no televisions in the bedrooms or in the dining room, but more importantly, I understood that in her family meals were the time to talk, to discuss your day, your projects, to express your ideas.

At her place meals were a ceremony during which you had to talk, and it would have been impolite not to. How could her way of life and ours be so symmetrically, so grotesquely opposite?

I saw this reversal at all levels: at our house a man had to have second and third helpings to show how hungry, and so how strong, and so how masculine he was, whereas at Elena's that would have been seen as greedy, unfitting and vulgar.

At our house meals had to be commented on, you took care of that, when we were finished you'd say One more meal the Krauts won't get their hands on. At Elena's place they never talked about the meal except to compliment Nadya on her cooking, a word or two in passing. They also didn't talk about their bodies, their stomachs, their bodily functions, the body had to disappear—and the strangest thing was that no one laid down these rules, they were just there.

But that's not what I want to talk to you about. I'm writing to tell you about the first time I felt my existence writhing inside me. It was one evening at Nadya's house and the mood was the same as always, ritualized, like in a dream you dream over and over again: the candles, the classical music far off in the kitchen, the bottles of wine around us, the silences between our comments—not like the silences I'd known when you'd gone to the café, Mom had finished cleaning up and fallen asleep on the sofa, exhausted, with the TV on and no sound, no it wasn't a silence like that, but a comfortable, privileged silence—even in silence there's no equality.

Then Nadya asked me And what do your parents do? If it's not too nosy, I mean. I haven't allowed myself to ask Elena.

I felt blocked, paralyzed. Something in me didn't want to tell her that you'd worked at the factory your whole life until the accident that broke your back and stopped you from returning, when you retrained as a street sweeper, or that my mother cleaned the bodies of the old and dying in the village, suddenly I couldn't say any of that. The shame was too great. I felt guilty about my story, how could I tell it, there, surrounded by these candles and this silence?

I turned things over in my head. I was sure that contrary

to what she'd said Elena had already told her, I couldn't lie
(later in Paris I would, when men I met in bars would ask me
what my parents did for a living, I'd tell them you're a lawyer
or a university professor, the shame would make me lie).

So I chose the opposite strategy. Rather than lie or avoid
the question, I said I come from a family of alcoholics and
prisoners. Nadya raised her eyebrows. I don't know if her surprise was genuine or feigned. I went on, I bet by now they're
watching some idiotic reality show, laughing their guts out
and eating their third packet of crisps. I bet by now my dad's
on to his eighth pastis and has his hands on his fat stomach.

I was ashamed by what I said, but I said it. You hated
crisps, you never ate them, you drank pastis, sure, and lots of
it, but I'd never put up with people calling you an alcoholic, it
was a judgmental word, even when Mom used it to talk about
you I got angry, and here I was using it too, I was exaggerating, not really lying but presenting reality in a way that would
disgust her, I knew it, it was as if when push came to shove
there was no difference between silence and exaggeration, as
if not answering and exaggerating were the same thing, the
same act, because in Nadya's presence both of them let me put
my past behind me.

I wanted to show Nadya that now I was on her side and
against this past, and to do so I had to denigrate this past as
much as possible. Nadya smiled a tight smile, I felt she was
getting ready for me to say that I wasn't serious. I hated myself
but I couldn't stop, it was too late, my words sickened me but
at the same time I must admit they comforted me, because
they reassured me about my place in the world. I was no longer like Mom and you, that's what I was implying to Nadya,

I'm not like them anymore. Nadya held my gaze, too long, far too long; she held mine to know if I was serious and I held hers to let her know I was.

She smiled again and said: Oh I'm sure you're exaggerating, I'm certain your parents are talking or wondering what you're doing tonight. That's what she said but in her eyes I felt like she was begging me: Tell me you're not exaggerating, tell me it's even worse than that.

I added: Oh they couldn't care less about me. And no, they're not talking. They never talk. What would they say to each other? They're watching TV like always.

Nadya raised her eyebrows. How awful. I've always hated TV. She refilled my glass, the red of the wine glistening in the candlelight, the candles glistening in my retina. Elena and her father were silent, they were listening to us, and in those moments when she, Nadya, focused her attention on me there was no noise, nothing but the city, far off in the night.

Nadya drew a long, resounding breath and we talked about something else. That was the first time I did that. Deep down I hated myself. I thought of you, of how much it would have hurt you to hear what I was saying, your disbelief perhaps, your question: Why are you saying this about us? I wanted so badly to be accepted by Nadya. I wanted so much to belong to her world. To belong to her world was to save myself from my childhood—is it possible to forgive me? I was suffering but later, when I went to sleep in the guest room next to Elena's room, I lay down and closed my eyes, appeased, feeling that I belonged a little less to my past.

I'M SORRY.

DESPITE EVERYTHING, I KNOW THAT MOM AND YOU were proud too, proud to have a son who was *getting on in life*, who was continuing with school, practically the only boy in the village who was, proud to have a son who stood a chance of entering the middle class.

Hurt and pride coexisted in you like two sides of the same emotion. When you went fishing on the weekend and one of your friends saw that I wasn't coming, that I was going to stay at home alone and he asked why, you said it was because I preferred to read and study, and I could hear the pride in your voice. I could hear your pride and how hard you tried to say it as casually as you could, as if it was unimportant, so your friends couldn't suspect you of thinking you were better than them.

Mom would ask me for photocopies of my report cards and go around the village with them, showing them to everyone she met, bragging that her son was "excelling at school" (it was so rare for anyone to continue with their studies that for her simply aiming to get your baccalaureate counted as "excelling"). The other women laughed at her, even to me they said Your mother's putting us to sleep with her stories, but she didn't listen to them, she kept at it, she felt stronger than these women, she was sure that the bits of paper she held in her hand were proof of her superiority.

She was getting back at all the women who'd thought they were better than her, the grocer who looked down on her when asked if she could pay the following day, the secretaries at the town council who disdained her because she had trouble expressing herself, she was using me to get her revenge, to show these women that they'd been wrong to think so little of her.

(It's not easy for me to recall all these images, I had to do an immense amount of memory work just to bring them to the surface, because for years I'd buried these scenes, which jarred so completely with the story I wanted to tell myself at the time, that of the son who succeeds against all odds, and above all against his family.)

Why didn't you ever say anything to me? The time I almost died of peritonitis during the school holidays and had to stay in the hospital for several weeks, you came to see me and gave me news magazines and chocolate. No one we knew ever read newspapers or magazines, you'd never bought any before. You weren't familiar with them, and because you had no idea you bought me staunchly right-wing publications, things I never read, things that Elena's family had taught me to hold in contempt. I thanked you and took them, and you said you'd chosen them because you knew I was interested in politics. There were also reports on the kings of France, you said, maybe that could help me at school.

That day in my hospital room I realized that maybe, sometimes, you thought about my life, my studies and my future.

I HARDLY SAW YOU ANYMORE. I SPENT MY EVENINGS AND nights at Elena's place. I'd known her for six months now and during the dinners at her home I felt more and more at ease. I didn't speak as well as she did, of course, I didn't know as much as she did, but I felt less intimidated and during the conversations about literature and the cinema (the most frequent) I talked about books I hadn't read, films or plays I hadn't seen (fake it till you make it, as the saying goes, play a role until it becomes your very being, and during those dinners at Elena's place that was just what I was doing, I was playing a role, hers, I was playing at being her, at talking about the things she talked about, saying words the way she said them, because I hoped to become like her by dint of imitation). Everything was changing in me, and paradoxically, because I was moving away from you, you were becoming more present in my life.

You were becoming a negative presence.

———

I went to the arthouse cinema with Elena and saw retrospectives of Todd Haynes, Gus Van Sant, Orson Welles.
When we came out I thought of you: my father's never done
this, he's never seen this. He'll never know who Gus Van
Sant is. In the evenings during meals at Nadya's place: he'll
never experience the texture of these dinners, the piano, the
candles, the conversations about painting, because even if he
had these candles or heard these notes, nothing in his being
has prepared him to experience their beauty. I didn't yet see in
this gap between my life and yours a sign of injustice or class
violence, but only that I was destined for a greater and more
beautiful life.

Yet despite everything my transformation was slower than
I'd hoped or imagined it would be. That became clear one
night when I was in Elena's room—a memory that overshad-
ows all the rest. Her parents and sister had gone to bed and
like almost every night I'd left the guest room on tiptoes to
go and sleep with her. For all those years her room was part
of the architecture and geography of my being; a small attic
with a garret window, poorly lit, hot in the summer. Elena was
smoking in front of the open window. That night she turned
to me: You know, I think it's time you learned how to eat, it'd
be better for you. The moment she said those words I felt my
body stiffen. I'd never thought about it explicitly, never spelled
it out to myself, but I knew exactly what she meant. I mean
it's for you, she went on, in front of other people you'll do better in life if you don't eat like a peasant. Or else you'll leave a
bad impression. I was silent. *Wait here, don't move.* She left the
room; I heard her going down the two flights to the ground

floor. She came back up with a plate, a knife and fork and half
a baguette. I watched her like a vision of my future. I tried not
to miss a thing, her breath, her flowing gestures.

She cut small pieces of bread no more than an inch or so
in length and placed them on the plate. Then she looked at
the pieces of bread, then at me, without saying a word, to see
if I'd understood. I nodded slightly to indicate that she should
go on. She whispered: *Here, like this*; she placed her hands on
the knife and fork and showed me how to hold them, where to
place the fingers on the handle, then she pricked the pieces of
bread with the fork and brought them delicately to her mouth.
That's how you hold them, not like this, she said, grasping the
knife and fork in her closed fists in a crude imitation of me
holding my cutlery. I looked at her fingers, trying to remember everything so no detail would slip from my memory. She
did it again, I watched her, then she gave me the knife and
fork and I tried to reproduce the same gestures. No, she whispered, not like that, put your hand like this. I listened to her,
Yes, that's right, she continued, like that, that's good. I had
the feeling that I was accelerating time, that I was learning in
a few minutes what her body had assimilated in fifteen years
through the contact with her family and the repetition of
meals over days and seasons. When there was no more bread
left she showed me how to place the knife and fork in the center of the plate, with the blade slipped between the tines of the
fork, balanced, the way her mother did. At every meal over the
next few days I tried to eat as Elena had shown me. The others
were eating and they thought that's what I was doing too, but
in fact I was working, learning a new body.

THE SCENE WITH THE KNIFE AND FORK IN ELENA'S ROOM made me realize that my past was everywhere in me, in the way I ate, but also in the way I walked, dressed and talked. My body told a different story from the one I wanted to create by force of will alone; it wasn't enough to know the names of novelists, to go to the cinema with Nadya and Elena or to talk about different things to become someone else. What I had been was written in my flesh, in my voice, in my movements, and I resolved to transform my very being. I swore I'd eradicate all the marks of what I'd been; I remembered the first week in Amiens when a girl had laughed at my northern accent after she heard me talking in the corridor. So I practiced. Every day I practiced saying words without an accent; I repeated them while I was walking in the street and at night before going to bed, I tried hard to control the contractions of my lips, tongue and throat when I spoke to Nadya and Elena, I had to focus on each word so as not to make a hash of it, I tried to imitate the posh accents in the films I saw with them (some people like Étienne, a new friend, noticed this transformation at school. Why are you speaking with that ridiculous accent? he said to me—even though he spoke the same way, as if getting it from your family was legitimate but acquiring it by choice and hard work was contrived and laughable).

When my concentration flagged while I was talking to others and a northern twang sounded in my words, I was filled with self-loathing and insulted myself in silence, calling myself a bumpkin and a yokel, the way I'd insulted myself as a child when someone called me a queer, repeating the insult to myself for hours on end as if the insulter had grafted the insult onto me, as if he'd had the power not only to insult me but also to force me to repeat the insult to myself for all eternity, as if the violence of the insult went hand in hand with a forced complicity. I despised myself but never gave up, I practiced all the time, day in, day out, in the shower, on the bus, *you have to get rid of your accent, you have to get rid of your accent*—I remember one evening when I was on the verge of tears trying to pronounce the word "jaune," or yellow, and say "zhone" and not "zhaan" as I'd always done, but I couldn't, my past was everywhere, in my mouth, in my tissue, in my muscles. I didn't understand how my mouth could be so rigid and so incapable of uttering a word, a tiny word, and my inability made my eyes well up.

Laughter, too: when I laughed with Romain during the first days at school he said my laugh was too loud, too jarring. Whenever I laughed with him in class he'd say Don't laugh so loud! I knew my laughter was bound up with my past.

No one had to spell it out to me, I could see that the world

THE ELENA EFFECT: BARELY TWO
YEARS SEPARATE THESE PHOTOS

was organized around binary principles: heavy/light, noisy/
quiet, fat/thin, visible/suggested, pushy/subtle, uncouth/distin-
guished, which are also class principles, and that I was always,
inevitably, on the less legitimate side of this dichotomy.

So I did with my laugh what I'd done with my accent: I
practiced. I decided to learn a new laugh through sheer willpower. Every day I stationed myself in front of the mirror and
practiced laughing differently, less loudly, less expressively, with
my mouth less wide open. I practiced laughing in a way that

was more in keeping with my new life, with my new world, with Elena and with the urgency of my metamorphosis. When I was with friends at school, Morgan, Julie or Étienne—the ones I spent the most time with apart from Elena—and they said something funny, I tried to laugh with my new laugh, even in the funniest moments when by definition you let your-self go and lose control I stayed focused and laughed with my new laugh, the one I'd invented in front of the mirror.

Little by little this artificial, mimed laughter became my laughter—and today when I hear it, on a video for example, I can't help hearing something fake. I hear the trace of its mak-ing, the long hours in front of the mirror with only myself as a witness, learning my life the way you learn a role in the theater. My whole life became an effort of concentration. I concentrated when I spoke, when I laughed, when I sneezed, when I ate, all of that became an exercise for me.

I was also doing sports for the first time, to lose weight. I went running in the forests behind the village, because with Elena I'd learned the value of taking care of your body. In one year I lost over ten kilos. I wanted to eat *light*, *organic*, *healthy* things. When I said those words they went straight to my head.

Elena dyed my hair to make me look more like her and put more distance between me and my former appearance; I invented an eye problem at the doctor's office so I could wear glasses like her—and it worked. With a slender body, long hair and glasses, I no longer looked like you at all.

When I came home on weekends I worked in the village bakery. I sold bread, baked pastries, and carried hundreds of baguettes from the oven to the shop. With the money I earned I went to the cinema with Elena or bought wine that I gave to Nadya when I had dinner with her family. That was another one of the gestures I adopted in my new life away from you: going to the wine shop before dinner and buying a bottle to offer as a gift, because Étienne had told me that you should never go to dinner empty-handed but bring flowers or wine instead—in the village there was no such rule, and if you did give someone something it was to make them happy, not because of some rule. I'd walk through Amiens holding the bottle of wine I was about to give Nadya and I liked that image of myself. I thought: you've made it, you have another life. One day I went to a department store and bought some clothes and shoes. I wanted to ditch my joggers and hoodies and buy jeans, polo shirts and shirts, clothes that suited my new way of talking and laughing, a long black coat that reached my knees, shoes we called city shoes in our family, black, with heels, that looked like they were made of suede.

I had a new voice, no accent—or so I thought—a new laugh, a new appearance. I looked at my reflection in the mirror and thought: you're someone else. Elena continued to participate in my transformation, she taught me to tie ties with Windsor knots, the ones she thought were the most elegant, and I wore them to school. The evening Nadya saw me in a tie she almost fell over in surprise: Well, well, Eddy, you're becoming gentrified. She didn't know that was the nicest thing she could have said to me, and in the days that followed I repeated it to myself until I just about went mad.

I DON'T THINK YOU CARED MUCH, BUT IN THE FIRST YEAR at the lycée my marks were average, often bad, because I didn't like studying and didn't know how to go about it, I had no idea how to study or how to learn. I could see that it wasn't just a question of understanding things, of what you knew or didn't know, but also of method. During all the years I lived with you I did my homework at the kitchen table, in the only shared room in the house. You watched TV, smoked, shrugged and said that school was useless, my brothers and sisters talked over each other while Mom prepared dinner at the same table where I was trying to finish my homework. The bedrooms didn't have desks, they were too small, and anyway since there were no doors the rooms were as noisy as the living room–kitchen. At school when I handed in my homework stained with grease and tomato sauce the French teacher laughed, Well, Mr. Bellegueule, at least we know what you had for dinner last night, and I laughed too.

At the lycée when I compared myself to Elena I had the impression that our attitude to schoolwork would separate us forever, despite the transformation I'd undertaken with her. It was hard for me to grasp the strength that gripped her body when she sat in front of a book or sheet of paper and filled it with her handwriting—the type of thing we'd always found laughable and affected at my old school and in the village. I alternated between phases of hard work and discouragement, but in both cases my results were mediocre at best. However, at the same time something else was coming home to me: in Elena's family everyone had studied, studying was a dimension of life that was almost as natural as eating or breathing. When I arrived in Amiens it had come as a surprise to me to see that for middle-class city children, even those with average marks or who didn't like school, studying was a matter of course, whereas in the village it could only be a feat of immense willpower, a struggle, and for those with average marks not studying was pretty much the order of the day.

So when I understood, no doubt as the sum of an infinite number of small moments, remarks and observations, that school was an absolute condition for my transformation, just as much as the clothes I wore, I began to apply myself with all my strength.

I imitated Elena, her way of living and studying. Seeing as I slept in her house, I had a room and a desk to work at. I'd lock myself in, write and rewrite my homework in the house that Nadya kept absolutely silent during study time, two or three hours a day.

In fact, for the first time I internalized the rhythm of this silence, its necessity, in my body, every day. It became a part of my biorhythm, something I'd never experienced because such a silence had never existed at home.

(Later, when I fell out with Elena and her family, Nadya said to me: You took advantage of everything we gave you. What does that mean, to take advantage of something? Didn't Elena also take advantage of what her mother gave to her? Her social background?

Are there people for whom taking advantage of what's given to them is legitimate, and others for whom it's a scandal, an expropriation?)

I was working at school, but still getting bad grades. I'd fallen too far behind in science and math in the village, and I could no longer catch up. Thanks to all the references I'd learned from Nadya and Elena I was better at French and history, and it became clear to me just how much your family environment can help with your studies.

Then during my second year in Amiens something changed. I had to select some subjects and eliminate others. I was able to drop science and math almost completely and focus on theater, literature, history and languages. I still didn't read, books and reading eluded me, but I continued to go to the cinema with Elena, and I even imitated her attempts at writing. She wanted to write; she wrote little sketches that she gave me to read and, without realizing it, in the days that followed I'd copy them almost word for word, thinking I was producing something original.

Thanks to all these elements—a growing familiarity with culture, a new study rhythm, the belief that school would save

me, dropping the subjects in which I was lagging behind—
I became more and more adapted to the school system. I was
progressing, and by the end of my second year in Amiens my
results were better than almost everyone in the class.

LISTEN.

It's night in Elena's room. I'm lying next to her. We sleep there together in her tiny bed almost every night, my body against hers. She's smoking. She's opened the window so her parents don't smell the smoke, and the cold of the night comes in and settles on our faces and arms.

It's two or three in the morning, her parents are asleep, we had dinner together and drank a lot of wine. I turn my head toward her, see the cigarette between her fingers, the smoke leaving her mouth and wafting up and out the window.

She asks me if I want a drag. I say yes with a self-assured voice, as if I've done it before. The cigarette passes from her lips to mine and I inhale the smoke. My body tries to cough as the smoke enters my lungs but I repress it and don't cough. I pass the cigarette back to Elena. She takes it without glancing at me, her eyes raised to the ceiling.

She says: Will we always stay together? I listen. I mean, you and I will never leave each other, right, we're bound by a pact.

I think when she says this I already know it's a teenage thing to say, and so does she, we both know that it's the kind of grand declaration you make when you're a certain age, in the night after drinking too much, but I don't mind, on the contrary.

I answer: Of course. We'll never leave each other.

I'm slightly ashamed because I can't make sentences as beautiful and as poetic as Elena does. My shame disperses in the smoke around us, it mingles with the night, mellowed by the wine in my veins. She continues: We'll live together and no one will understand our relationship because it won't be like theirs.

She sketches our life: I'll be a journalist and you'll be a history teacher. We'll live in a big, ramshackle house with thousands of books stacked on top of each other. In the evening we'll listen to classical music and open a bottle of wine, and we'll lie down and listen to the music together. Sometimes we'll dance. No one will understand.

Just as she finishes a new song comes from the speakers on the shelves between the books. I say Want to dance? We've never done it before, she's uncomfortable with her body, she never dances, but I ask her to and she says yes, I get up and take her hand and dance with her, in the middle of her cluttered room under the roof, and we dance for a long, long time, just us and the music around us, in the night, as if nothing existed at that moment but our two bodies against each other, no history, no past, no fear, no memories, no tomorrow.

———

I'm telling you this because when I reread what I've written so far, I see that I'm inevitably selecting certain moments in my story and forgetting others. There are things I don't know or don't want to tell, and I don't want you to think that for me Elena was nothing but a tool for relearning myself, I don't want you to imagine that I used her to get where I wanted to go. If that's the takeaway from what I've written I've failed completely. I loved Elena, I loved her more than anything (even writing these words I feel stupid). It wasn't a romantic relationship, there was no desire between us—I desired men, that was clear, even if I hid it—but what we had was more than friendship. I loved her.

AND THEN THERE WAS MY NAME. MOM SAYS THAT WAS the hardest thing for you in my transition, and it was the only time she mentioned how you reacted to what I was becoming.

One evening I arrived at Elena's place at eight o'clock, as planned. I was wearing one of my new shirts, I'd washed it to get rid of the shoppy smell but I hadn't ironed it, and as I walked I pulled on the fabric with all my might to try to get rid of the creases. I rang the bell and Nadya opened the door.

Hello, Édouard.

I didn't move. It was the first time; I had no idea why she'd called me a name that wasn't mine. She saw the surprise on my face,

You don't mind me calling you Édouard, do you? That's what Eddy's short for, isn't it? Eddy isn't really a name, and I prefer Édouard, I think it's much more elegant. Is that all right with you?

Eddy. That was the name you had chosen, because of the American films and TV shows you liked, that's what the bad guys and thugs were called and that's why you liked it, it was a masculine name, a tough name. For Nadya it wasn't a name at all. I told her I didn't mind. She was christening me. She didn't know that one day this name would be mine forever, and that when I was far from Amiens it would appear on my ID.

She asked me to come into the living room where Elena and her sister were sitting

Édouard's here

Elena looked at her mother, then at me

Édouard?

She shrugged. Okay, fine, Édouard. From that evening on Elena never called me Eddy again, that very night after dinner, lying next to me on her bed, she told me that she agreed with her mother, that Édouard suits me better than Eddy, that it's the name of a prince, a king.

Nadya asked Elena's little sister to play a piece on the piano, Why don't you play something to welcome Édouard to our home? Elena's sister got up, sat down at the piano and started to play. Music filled the room, beautiful, deep, and as I listened my new name echoed inside me.

The first person I told was Mom. She'd just split up with you, barely a week before, she'd stuffed all your things in bin bags and thrown them on the pavement, telling you never to come back. I told her from that day on I wanted her to call me Édouard. She laughed, Monsieur Édouard is a gentleman now, always calling me Monsieur this, Monsieur that to make fun of me—and then she talked about something else. I don't know if she was hurt or if she thought it was a short-lived whim, a teenage rebellion.

Now that I think about it, maybe when she told me you'd been hurt by me changing my name she was also talking about herself, maybe she talked about your feelings to avoid talking about her own.

IMAGINARY CONVERSATION IN FRONT OF A MIRROR

Actually one thing is a bit of a mystery . . . If you were so different to start out with, how did you come to terms with Elena and her world so fast? Why weren't you discouraged by your failed attempts to be like her?

As I've said, most of the time when I was alone in the village and at school there it was because no one wanted to play with the boy everyone thought was gay. During the breaks I'd wander around the playground. Sometimes I managed to worm myself into this or that group of children, but I felt that my presence weighed on them.

I remember times when I'd spend the entire break pretending I was looking for something in my schoolbag or locker, so the others would think that if I was alone it was because I was busy, and that if I'd wanted to I could have played with them. Then this pretense became too difficult to keep up. I couldn't look for something in my schoolbag or locker every day for the whole year, nobody would believe that. So when there was no way to do anything else I started spending the breaks at the school library. I realized that if I wanted to I could spend all my time there, it was empty most of the time, so I'd sit there with a book I didn't read, pretending to be reading without anyone suspecting that it was because I'd been excluded.

You spent months in the library without reading a thing? Didn't the others think that was odd?

With time I got closer to the school librarian. I think she must have been a bit bored and was happy to have someone to talk to. Her name was Pascale Boulnois. Little by little I got into the habit of going there and chatting with her on every break, and when I had a bit of free time. She'd talk to me about books, but not only, also about history and politics. She and I became friends in a way. Even though I was eleven and she was thirty-five we had a sort of understanding, I think you could call it friendship. When she went on holiday in the summer she'd send me postcards and text messages. Getting them was like a sort of revenge against my family, an embryonic form of what I'd feel later with Elena and Nadya. I told myself that I belonged to another world, and that I was more like her than I was like my own family. That's also how I started to change. Because I had no choice. I started going to the library to hide, because I didn't have any friends on the playground, it's as silly and anecdotal as that. I think the prolonged contact with this older, more cultivated woman triggered a metamorphosis in my way of being and thinking, that she prepared me in some way, intellectually and psychologically, for the meeting with Elena a few years later, and that's why I got along with Elena so naturally. And Pascale Boulnois also encouraged me to go to the lycée, although that was unusual for someone from a school like mine.

And what about in the village? You mentioned the village just now.

The astonishing thing is that exactly the same thing happened there. On Wednesday afternoons when there was no school, the other children on my street went to play football and didn't ask me to come along. As it turned out, a library had just opened in the village, and I'd go there. It had been set up by the town council in a small loft, hardly more than an alcove. I went there so I wouldn't be alone, and there too I struck up a friendship with the librarian, Stéphanie Morel. Like Pascale Boulnois, she talked to me about politics and the world. At the time I used to record myself singing on cassette tapes, and I'd get her to listen. I dreamed of being a famous singer, I watched all the reality shows and singing competitions. She encouraged me, and told me I was going to become famous one day. She was thirty, I was ten or eleven and she became my friend.

May I digress for a bit? One day the mayor decided to fire her, and that was one of the darkest days of my childhood. I was still a child, but I drew up a petition, demanding that the mayor keep Stéphanie in her job, and went around the village for several days, knocking on every door, at every house. I'd go back to my parents' house at ten or eleven in the evening with my stack of signatures, my shoes caked with mud because at the time, in the early 2000s, many of the streets were still made of dirt and hadn't yet been paved over, as if we lived in a different age from the rest of the world. When I was sure I'd knocked on every door without exception—I'd collected several hundred signatures, more than half the village—I put the petition through the mayor's letter box and took another copy to Stéphanie. She cried and told me it was too late and I cried with her, in her living room beside the fireplace that smelled of ashes.

I hate stories of childhoods saved by books and libraries, I find them naive. But I have to say that these two women, Pascale Boulnois and Stéphanie Morel, were among the ones who saved me, without whom I'd never have been able to escape and invent a new life. Without them, I could never have become close to Elena.

EMOTIONS CONTAIN WITHIN THEM THE POSSIBILITY OF their own mutation: love into jealousy, resentment into hatred, worry into dread, the longing for vengeance into a quest for revenge. With time—in particular during my last year at the lycée—when I was better integrated into the world of Amiens, something shifted, a barely perceptible mutation took place within me: I no longer wanted to be like the others, I wanted to go further than them. I wanted to show them that I could do things none of them could do and achieve things they'd never have thought possible. When I said that to Elena she encouraged me: *Show them you're better than they are.*

Here's what happened: the longing that had brought me to Amiens, namely to be avenged for my childhood, turned into a quest for revenge—no longer just against my childhood but against the whole world. When I thought of the future, I no longer thought just about you or our family and setting myself apart from the world we had shared. I wanted to set myself apart from everyone else as well.

It was enough for me to meet someone new and hear them talk about their ambitions for me to think: *I must go further.* When a girl at school told me she dreamed of going to Oxford, saying it was one of the greatest universities in the world, I spent the evening reading about Oxford on the Internet and promising myself that I too could get in if I wanted, that by doing so I'd surprise Elena, Nadya, all my friends in Amiens, and that their surprise would put my whole life in a new light.

One question took center stage in my life, it focused all my thoughts and occupied every moment when I was alone with myself: how could I get this revenge, by what means? I tried everything. Like in my previous school I joined all the clubs and associations, the book club, the haiku club, the film workshop. I wanted to exist, and to exist meant to stand out. When one student out of more than a thousand got to write a speech about Madeleine Michelis, the member of the French Resistance after whom our lycée was named, and read it to the whole school, I volunteered and was selected. It's silly, but I felt important. I was the one who'd written it, and not one of the thousand other students who'd been born with far more opportunities, a general culture and a chance to learn new languages. I got elected to the student council and other committees, and I felt intoxicated as I entered the meeting rooms.

When the dates of the baccalaureate exams were announced, I set my mind to beating everyone else—you don't know anything about all of this, or what was going on inside me at that time in my life. In the two or three months that led up to the exams I studied as hard as I could, late into the

night, at lunchtime, in the mornings on the bus. I spent my
weekends with Elena at the public library. Friends invited me
to go for walks in the park, it was spring, the weather was
nice, and I took a kind of pride in turning them down, saying that I preferred to study. The morning the results were
announced I went to wait with Elena in the McDonald's near
the school. She was afraid of disappointing her parents, I was
afraid my dreams of revenge would be dashed. We drank coffee from plastic cups, she held my hand under the table and
stroked my hair, whispering It'll be okay, it'll be okay. When
we got to the school I looked for our names on the billboards
outside and saw that I'd passed all the exams and so had she.
I'd passed with distinction, we shouted for joy and she hugged
me. Nadya said we could throw a little party at their place that
evening, and during the party I decided to enroll in history
at the university, like Elena, to imitate her. I was going to
become a university student, the word student cut me off radically from you and our world. In the village saying *I'm a university student* was like saying *my country house* or *my cleaning
lady*, expressions that marked a clear, definitive, uncrossable
boundary—and I was passing over to the other side.

ABOVE ALL THERE WAS POLITICS. DURING MY SECOND year in Amiens I'd joined a party on the far left of the political spectrum. I'd done it in reaction to my childhood and the village, and to keep putting distance between us. In the village most people voted for parties on the far right, and everywhere you went—in the bakery, on the church square, in the streets—you heard it nonstop: France? This isn't France anymore, it's Africa, and in my metamorphosis I'd wanted to reject all of these ideas that my evenings at Nadya's had taught me to see as simplistic. Of course I'd done so because of my disgust for injustice and poverty, and because I'd felt them in my own body. But the third reason, the least noble, was that politics allowed me to exist in the eyes of others, and to take my desire for revenge a step further. I'd have preferred to say that my political commitment was linked purely and simply to my revolt against the world, but that would be a lie. What I have to tell you is by definition the hardest thing to admit. A few months before the baccalaureate exams, a protest movement against the government was formed; I took part, organized rallies and demonstrations, and put the different lycées in the city in touch with each other to coordinate our strategies. Little by little I became one of the leaders of the movement. I took the mike and spoke to hundreds of people before the demonstrations started, I carried banners at the head of the processions, the local newspapers interviewed me—and then one day I was invited to defend my views on television, when you were still living with Mom, just before she kicked you out of the house. It was a regional TV show watched by a lot of the people in the village, including our whole family.

I told you that I'd been invited and that I'd accepted, and you were faced with a dilemma: you hated my leftist commitment because it was the opposite of your worldview—you weren't stupid, you understood that one of my objectives was to set myself apart from you—but the TV had always been the center of our lives, it fascinated us. It was what helped us fight boredom, what connected us to the world, and because of the power it exerted over us you couldn't help but feel a kind of respect and admiration for the people you saw on the screen.

When I told you I'd been invited I saw the emotion in your eyes. No doubt you thought your son had made it, and gone further than you could ever have imagined. He was going to be on television, the neighbors were going to see him. So despite everything you hated about my commitment, you nodded your approval.

Mom told me the rest. On the evening of the debate you invited two or three of your friends to come and watch me with you. You'd bought some pastis and cheap crackers. You'd arranged the chairs in a semicircle in the living room, facing the screen like in the cinema, Mom said, and you hadn't stopped smiling to yourself all day long.

In the evening your buddies arrived. They sat down, you served them drinks and you all waited.

As for me, I was escorted into the television studio and taken to a small dressing room where I was made up. I was trembling with emotion to be in this situation, to be someone who was being made up in a studio, I never thought I'd come this far—I was also thinking along those lines, I failed to see that it was only a regional program—and I think for a moment you and I were seeing eye to eye.

But when the program began, right from the word go I started talking about undocumented lycée and university students who were being expelled from France, and about the racism of the French state. I'd prepared this digression that afternoon, when I was thinking about what I could say. I'd been invited to talk about something else, but I told the presenter that I had to talk about undocumented migrants first, and I came back to the topic in almost all of my statements. I was trembling but I tried not to show it.

Mom said you stopped smiling when I started to speak. She said you frowned and your face turned purple. She said you left the TV set on for a while, as if you wanted to give me a chance, the time to understand what I was saying, what I was doing to you, and then you got up, turned it off and said, doing your best to sound casual, Let's not watch this drivel, we might as well just talk.

I'd hurt you. Your buddies Gébé and Titi saw that but they

didn't say anything. They knew you'd invited them to see the
program. You tried to sound as if everything was normal but
you spoke too fast, your gestures were jerky, there was something strange in your attitude.

I came home late, almost as night was falling (I don't know
why I didn't go to Elena's), the house was filled with the smell
of Mom's fried food, the stench of fuel oil and the noise of the
TV. You came up to me, grabbed me by the collar and said
Why'd you do that? Why'd you make an ass of me like that,
talking about undocumented migrants crap?

(TO BE FAIR, I MUSTN'T FORGET TO SAY THAT IF YOU WERE against my political commitment it wasn't just because it was diametrically opposed to your own worldview, but also because I took part in illegal demonstrations and was often beaten and gassed by the police. You were afraid that my activism would get me into trouble with the authorities, and that because of it everything I was doing to move up in the world could come to nothing and all my effort would be in vain. I know that because when I came back from a march with bruises on my skin or stickers on my clothes saying Down with Capitalism, Our Lives Are Worth More Than Their Profits, Freedom for the Palestinian People or Racist France, you'd say: What, you want a criminal record? You want to get kicked out of school? and there was less anger than concern in your voice.)

IN ANY CASE WELL BEFORE THE TV SHOW—AS EARLY AS the first weekends after I'd started spending time at Elena's place—it had become almost impossible for me to go back to the village. And things were getting worse and worse. I'd changed too much. My life in Amiens was everywhere in my body, Elena's presence colonized everything I did and said.

One day, inevitably, this impossibility led to a breaking point. I was having dinner with Elena, her sister and her parents. It was before I entered university, school had ended and we'd just received our exam results. There were candles, the table was decorated with flowers and small bronze statues, classical music played in the background—mostly Brahms's *Requiem*, Elena's father's favorite music. I'd come from Mom's house that evening, after going back to the village for a couple of days to earn some money at the bakery.

Elena's sister was telling us about her drawings when Nadya, who was passing behind me, asked Édouard, do you smoke? Sorry for asking, it's just that your clothes smell of tobacco. I don't remember if I blushed. It was the smell of Mom's cigarettes, the smoke had permeated my sweater. No, no, I said to Nadya, I've just come from my mom's place and she smokes a lot (tones of Brahms's *Requiem*, the sound of the instruments mixing with our voices). Nadya raised her eyebrows: She doesn't smoke in the room you're in I hope? I said that she did, that ever since I was born she'd smoked thirty cigarettes a day in the same room I was in, that you did too for years before Mom kicked you out, that I had no memory of a time when my parents didn't smoke, and that my older brother and sister also smoked—Mom had tried to stop them but you said it was up to them to decide, they had the right. Nadya's expression went from surprise to indignation, then disgust, You mean you breathed in the smoke of more than a hundred cigarettes a day as a child? I said yes. I'd never really thought about it before, while I was living with Mom and you it was perfectly normal, just one of the things that made the atmosphere in our house what it was, like the TV that stayed on even when no one was watching it. Nadya asked me again, Really? and I felt a new sort of anger rising in me. I nodded, I've been inhaling that much smoke since the day I was born. How dreadful, Elena's mother shrieked, do you know that children whose mothers smoked while pregnant and exposed them to cigarette smoke stand a far greater chance of developing cancer as adults? I'd never inflict that on my children!

We talked about something else, but all evening the anger continued to pulse through my veins, under my skin. The next week when I went back to the village to work and Mom lit up a cigarette I asked her to go out into the backyard to smoke. She looked at me as if I was crazy and said, Who does the little shit think he is, this is my home and I can do what I want. When she said that I stomped my foot and shouted, No! You're smoking outside! I told her she had no right to smoke indoors. She looked at me in surprise; she didn't understand why smoking next to me was suddenly such a problem when I'd never mentioned it before, when for sixteen years it had never been an issue. I could no longer stop myself. I told her that because of her my lungs were poisoned before I was ten, it's true, after the conversation with Nadya I'd read articles on the Internet, I told her that she was egotistical, I shouted it, I shouted that she was a bad mother, unable to raise children, and that wasn't the only thing, I was also angry that she'd called me a little shit, I wasn't used to such language anymore, Nadya never said things like that to her daughters, since I'd met Elena things that had seemed normal to me in my childhood all of a sudden seemed violent and aggressive from one day to the next, since I'd got to know Elena I looked back over my childhood and all I could see was a field of ruins and violence, as if I was living the violence of my childhood ten years after the fact—but when I said the words bad mother to Mom she blew up and shouted I've raised five kids, you're not going to tell me how to raise kids, I've got five kids and they're all healthy and polite, except for you now you think you're something, I don't know what, but I didn't let her finish, I didn't want to, I shouted Stop!!!!! I know what you're going to say, I shouted, Stop it, you're always saying the same thing, I can't take it anymore, I shouted, It's as if you only know ten sentences and keep repeating them over and over again, I despised her but I couldn't control myself, it was too late, I couldn't stop, I felt the tears running down my cheeks as I went on and yet I wasn't sad, they weren't tears of sadness but of rage, Because of you I'm going to fucking die, I said, you made me breathe in your smoke for my whole childhood, do you have any idea what you did to me, you ruined me, you ruined my body, plus you never taught me a thing, you never got me to read a book or took me to a museum, it's because of you that I can't get my act together in Amiens, it's because of you that I'm clueless compared to everyone else, it's because of you that I'm useless, and on top of all that you ruined my health, I said the most tragic, hurtful things I could think of, but I wasn't thinking, I didn't choose to say them, they just came out of my mouth, I said You're not a mother anyway, you're not a mother, you don't deserve to be a mother, I wish so much that Nadya was my mother and not you, she's so intelligent and so much better than you, why are you my mother and not her why was I born into this family and that's when she screamed Stop!!!!!!!!!!!!!!!!!!!!!!!!!!!!!!! She'd never screamed like that, so loud, and for so long. She came up and started punching me, not slapping but punching, clenching her fists and slugging me with all her strength, all her rage, without aiming, I can't stand you all anymore, she screamed, I can't stand this shitty life you'll never let me go you'll never let me go I'll never be happy with shitheads like you, and I shouted Stop, stop fucking hitting me, you're such a fucking lunatic, I hate you, I hate you, I don't want you to be my mother, tears and shouting, tears and shouting. After a while she stopped, panting for breath. I was crying, my arms in front of my face to ward off her blows. She was crying too. She looked at me like a monster.

AFTER THAT CLASH I REALIZED I COULDN'T GO BACK TO
the village on weekends.

I'd become someone else.

One night, this someone else who I'd become is lying on
Elena's bed, beside her, staring up at the ceiling in the darkness. He thinks about his childhood home. In the silence of
the room, next to Elena who's sound asleep, with her breath
on his face, he thinks: It's over. He thinks: I can't do it anymore it's over I can't go back there anymore it has to be over.

He tries not to make any sudden movements, he feels the
inside of his body and the surface of his skin twitching as they
always do on these evenings when, lying in bed, he projects
himself into a future life, as if his body was too eager for that
future and needed to move to make it happen as quickly as
possible, as if the movement, the friction of his cells and the
oxygen around him could speed up time.

Concentrating so as not to move a muscle and not wake Elena up he thinks, he can't help but think: I can't go back there anymore because going back is becoming what I was I can't do that I have to find a solution anything I can't go on like this it's over it has to be over it has to end.

He'd like not to have to go back to his parents' house, or rather to his mother's house since his father left, not to see her anymore. Not just because of the arguments. He thinks that continuing to see his family will prevent him from going through with his transformation. When he returns to the village he feels that he reverts to the manners and attitudes of his past, he becomes like he was, much more easily than he'd like to admit, and he's afraid, afraid to think all his efforts at changing have only produced a superficial result, afraid to think he's only learned to play a role and in reality somewhere under the surface of his skin he's remained the same, afraid also to think he's struggled so hard and in spite of that the past is still in his life, that he hasn't got rid of it completely.

Over the next few days he continues to think in this direction. He talks to Elena and she suggests he could try to find a job at the big theater in Amiens, the Maison de la Culture d'Amiens. A lot of students work there, she says, it's not too difficult, all you have to do is open the doors of the theater, welcome the guests and tear their tickets, then sit in the auditorium and make sure that everything goes smoothly during the performances, meaning those who work there get to see the shows for free for the entire season, that's why students want the job, it doesn't tire them out, they can save their energy for their studies and see all the shows they want. With his salary, she says, he'll be able to rent a small studio.

The very same day he gets to work, writes up a résumé, prints it out, puts on his best shirt and tie with the Windsor knot he learned from Elena, his black jacquard sweater with blue checks and fine white lines, and walks to the Maison de la Culture to submit the résumé he's just put together.

On his way to the theater his excitement mounts, he already sees himself leading a new life, no longer seeing his family, breaking all ties with them and living in a tiny room under the roof with Elena. He imagines the artistic life he'll share with her, the plays and classical music concerts he'll be able to see for free thanks to his work, he sees himself falling asleep in his tiny room, without a family, without any other family than Elena, and without realizing it he smiles. He thinks: I'd give anything to have that job, I'd give anything to have it, such a banal sentence seen from the outside and with years of distance, but the moment he thinks it nothing can give him so much strength, nothing is more powerful, nothing better conveys his desire than this sequence of words.

He arrives at the theater and asks at the box office where he should hand in his résumé. The woman behind the counter is cold, she hardly looks at him, she must think he's just one of the fifty or sixty theater students she'll see that day, she keeps her face fixed on her screen and says: Drop it here, I'll pass it on. Then she adds: To be honest we're not looking for anyone—her name is Christiane; later on, when Édouard works there with her, when he fulfills his dream, he'll realize that she's not this cold, hard woman but a gentle, funny, generous person. But for now he doesn't know that, for now he doesn't know anything.

He's not like the others, Édouard would like to shout, he's not like the hundred or so lycée and university students she'll see that day, he'd like to spell out his journey—the social journey he's already put behind him just to be here, in front of her, his struggles, his efforts, he'd like to make her understand that his mere presence there today is already the result of a fierce struggle, and just as these thoughts cross his mind, as the woman at the box office is still staring at her screen, another woman appears through a door behind the counter, a small, slender blond woman with short hair and an ease of movement that makes Édouard feel as if his own body were crooked.

The woman at the counter says to the one who's just come in: Ah, Babeth, hi.

They kiss on the cheek as if he weren't there. When Babeth moves, the scent of a soft, delicately sweet perfume wafts in the air.

The woman at the counter picks up the sheet of paper that Édouard has just given her and says to Babeth, Oh this is for you, this young man has just dropped it off. Babeth glances over at Édouard as if she hadn't noticed his presence, he does his best to stand up straight, still feeling crooked faced with the poise and delicacy of the woman in front of him, as if his posture wasn't a thing in its own right but a relation to other postures, as if the position of his body wasn't defined by itself but by its relation to other bodies, he tries to straighten and

Babeth smiles and says So you want to join our team. Yes please, he'd like to shout, take me I beg you, I'm not like the others, she's his only hope, he'd like to say, if she doesn't accept him it could be the start of his downfall and everything he's done so far will come to nothing, he'll have to go back to the village and maybe work in the factory like his father and grandfather and great-grandfather before him, who knows, such things happen, he knows they do, a downfall has to start somewhere, maybe without this job he'll have to work as a waiter in a bar and the strain and difficulty of the job will wear him out and because of that he won't succeed in his studies and without a diploma he'll have to go back to the village and get a job in the factory, or try to get by doing odd jobs since the factory has all but closed down, or work as a cashier at the supermarket like his cousin, things like that aren't rare, they happen, he knows it, it's possible, the thoughts run through his head, he's afraid of this steady downfall, it's a palpable risk. Instead he smiles and says: Yes, I love the theater more than anything else in the world, I'd like to work here so much.

He doesn't know if it's because of his answer or the look on his face, maybe because of his intonation, maybe she's a mind reader and has heard all the things he's just screamed inside him, she says to him, Come into my office, we'll talk.

He'd like to shout for joy in the immense entrance, he'd like to look at the woman in the box office who'd been so cold at first and who'd later become his friend, for now he'd like to say to her: Take that, he feels tall as he crosses the foyer behind Babeth, the sound of her heels on the smooth stone floor, but he controls himself, he thinks: it's not over yet, the ordeal isn't finished yet, it hasn't started, he'd like to tell Babeth how elegant, how beautiful, how majestic she is, he'd like to flatter her into liking him and giving him the job (Elena always made fun of his obsession with being liked, his obsession with other people, she called him an eternal flatterer, she didn't understand that he wanted to be liked because he wanted to survive, because he was afraid of the downfall).

Why was Babeth so nice to him that first time, why did she ask him back to her office when she received dozens of résumés like his every day? Maybe she'd seen him visit the theater with his lycée, maybe she recognized his face, but that's not a good enough explanation.

Why did she decide to protect him, and why in the years that followed, when he'll work in the theater, will she treat him almost like a son, caring about everything he does, his life, his studies, his health, his happiness, always encouraging him to go further, to do more, to *become someone* as she said, always regarding him as different from the others, excusing his lateness and slip-ups, whereas at times she'll be too harsh with all the rest? Had she read his story on his face?

In her office she offers him a cup of coffee. She sits down, her legs crossed, her chest somewhat raised, her body once again slightly bending Édouard's own, and says: So you love the theater?

He says yes. He says that he studied theater at his lycée, that he did nine or ten hours of theater a week and wants to become an actor, he says he doesn't want to bore her with his life but for him the theater has always been more than an art, it's been an instrument for reinventing his life, because thanks to the theater he was the first person in his family to go to a lycée and thanks to it he's learned that it's possible to play roles, to create a distance between himself and his life, his imposed life, his past, his family history, the theater let him understand that if he wants to be something else or someone else, no matter, then he has to play at it until he becomes that someone, he's understood that there is nothing else but roles. She looks at him, impressed, silent. He hears her breath, very light. He wonders if his declaration wasn't a little ridiculous, a little too proclamatory, maybe he talked too much, went too far. His heart pounds in his chest, he's afraid she'll hear even that, he tries to redeem himself and says: Sorry, maybe it's silly what I said.

She breathes in gently, smiles and says No not at all why should it be silly, I don't see what's silly about being passionate. What's silly is the absence of passion. He can't quite interpret the signs, he doesn't know if she's saying this out of politeness, out of pity for this poor lost boy or if she really thinks it. But the smile on her face reassures him, it's not a normal smile, it's not a polite or mocking smile, it's an embracing smile, that's what he thinks, Babeth's smile is less like a smile than like one body embracing another.

All of a sudden she puts on a more severe expression, as if now she was the one playing a role, and asks: But are you a serious young man? You know I'm a tough nut, I won't hesitate to fire someone if they're not doing their job, I have responsibilities, she says, I'm not here to make friends, I'm here to make sure that this great theater maintains its prestige, but strangely enough her face contradicts her, it betrays her, she says she's not a friend but when she says it her face has all the signs, all the shades of friendship.

He answers that he's already held jobs, in summer camps, that he often works in the bakery in the village where he grew up, he's only just seventeen but he's already worked a lot, he'd like to add: I swear. He's just saying this when a man comes in, his body oddly animated by the same movements as Babeth's, as if their very bodies were determined by the position they occupy in the theater, and as he comes up to her with a pale blue file in his hands she says: Christophe, this is Édouard, he'll be working with us from now on.

*   *   *

The following Monday he's asked to come to the Maison de la Culture to sign his contract. On his way there he thinks that this signature is one more milestone in his life. He's going to work in a theater; no one in his family would have had the possibility or even the idea of doing that. In her office Babeth hands him the contract to sign and initial page by page. She shows him the black trousers and purple shirt he'll wear, which she's just bought at Burton, a shop in the center of town, still wrapped in a thin layer of plastic, and then takes him to the small room hidden behind the box office. The walls in this narrow, windowless space are lined with lockers for the ushers—

that's the name of his new job. She points to the one assigned to him and says she'll put a label with his name on it; then, after a second or two of silence, she clears her throat, Do you want me to put Eddy or Édouard? When we met you introduced yourself as Édouard, but I saw it says Eddy on your ID. And without letting him answer she adds, It's up to you, we can write the name you want, here everyone's free to do as they please.

He'd like to take her in his arms (I realize today that writing my story is writing the story of these women who saved me one after the next, Pascale Boulnois, Stéphanie Morel, Aude Detrez, Madame Coquet, Elena, Babeth, and that my story is the story of their will and generosity).

I prefer Édouard if possible, he whispers, barely audible, but immediately adds that of course if it's too complicated, since it's not the name on his contract or his ID she can put Eddy, he says he'll understand, there's no problem, he's aware of the administrative constraints, he apologizes for his answer, as if he was apologizing for his metamorphosis, and as always Babeth smiles and cuts him short Are you deaf or what, I've just said it's up to you. Besides, I think Édouard suits you better, it matches the softness of your face.

Three or four times a week now he crosses the city to work at the theater. There he meets Léa, Satine, Lucas, Alexandre and Cécile, all artists in the making or students who work there to pay for their studies. For him they're mirrors of what he'll become, he's filled with pride to be surrounded by artists and people who go to see plays and concerts, who read essays and novels in their free time; in the process of change those around us are as important as what we'll become, and

he compares his colleagues at the theater with his father's buddies, the guys who used to come over to his parents' place in
the late afternoon when he was a kid to watch TV and drink
pastis.

When he arrives at the theater he goes into the changing
room behind the box office and sees the seven letters of his
new name on the tag printed by Babeth.

Édouard is no longer just a name that Elena calls him
and that he says, it's no longer just a sound that exists in the
voices of Nadya, Elena and himself, it has now been inscribed
in the objectivity of the world on this tag stuck to his locker,
printed out, it's possible to touch it, grab hold of it. He thinks
to himself that while a sound is not proof, a name tag is. His
metamorphosis is visible, here, for all humanity to see.

A MEMORY: WE'D GONE TO THE SEASIDE ON A SCHOOL trip with the lycée. I was with Elena. Images of northern France, everything was gray and cold, rain was falling on the sea, even the sand was gray. We were walking together, away from the group. You coming in? she said, and I ran beside her down to the sea, my body beside hers, my hand in hers, our laughter. She ran in and I ran in with her, both of us fully dressed, the water was icy cold. Even in the sea I didn't let go of her hand.

On the way back when the adults who were accompanying us saw our sopping wet clothes they were so surprised it didn't even occur to them to scold us.

NOW I HAD TO FIND A FLAT.

I started looking but everything was too expensive, the money from the Maison de la Culture wasn't enough, I'd have to move in with someone else; I bumped into Cynthia almost by chance on one of my last weekends in the village and she told me she had a project, she was planning to move out and go live in Amiens. She was my age, and she was the only other person in the village who was starting university (she'd give up toward the end of her first year, as if the curse on the village always ended up striking those who wanted to escape).

She needed to find something near the university. So I said we could move in together and she accepted; I looked on the Internet and found a flat with a large bedroom on Boulevard Carnot, between the theater where I worked and the law faculty where Cynthia would be studying.

I told her she could have the bedroom and I'd sleep in the living room, I'd called the owners and they'd agreed to let us

have the flat, I didn't want to wait a day longer. They told me
they had to paint the walls before giving us the keys and I said
I'd do it if it meant we could move in straight away (I didn't
know how to paint and it would be a disaster).

I was in a hurry. I dreamed of a life with Elena in that
flat, the films I'd watch with her, the conversations we'd have.
Above all I dreamed of putting into practice at my place the
new aesthetic of existence that I'd learned at hers, with her
family: wine with dinner, starters before meals, classical music
(I'd bought recordings of the Brahms and Mozart requiems).
I wanted to experience them not only as a guest, I wanted
them to be part of my life, my daily routine, even when I was
alone, I don't know why but it was important to me, it made
a difference when I thought about it.

Cynthia let me take care of everything, I called the owners
and barely a week later I moved in. I'd bought a sofa, a table
and two small chairs.

*   *   *

I remember this moment as one of limitless freedom. I'd invite
the new people I'd met at university back to my place, along
with Julie, Étienne and other friends from the lycée. When we
went out to bars on the weekend and people asked me what I
did, I'd say "I'm a history student" and the words gave me a
naive euphoria, when I said them I was in two places at once,
I came out of my body and could hear myself speak, I never
believed I'd be able to say such things one day.

In fact during the year we shared the flat Cynthia would hardly be there at all, and I'd have it to myself. She was failing at law school and life in the city seemed too much for her, the village was everywhere under her skin and prevented her from enjoying life anywhere else. She drove back to her father's place in the evenings after her classes, I practically never saw her.

Elena and I had the flat to ourselves and a new life could really start.

Elena showed me films by directors I didn't know, we watched them on my computer, Werner Herzog, Orson Welles, Jane Campion, Pedro Almodóvar, she'd come and get me in the evening and we'd go to the cinema or the theater. She gave me books that I piled up on the floor because I didn't have the money to buy shelves, I prided myself on my poverty, I was an intellectual, a bohemian.

When I woke up in the morning I'd tell myself that I'd triumphed over my childhood, over the beatings, the insults, the humiliation. I looked around the flat and said to myself: I've won.

ONLY ONE THING WAS MISSING, SOMETHING I THOUGHT about every day during the four years I spent in Amiens. Above all I'd escaped from the village for one reason: my desire, and the hatred of that desire in the village. My attraction to other boys and men had always been clear to me. I'd been able to lie to myself and to you but I never had any doubts, all the times I lied to myself about what my body wanted I knew it was a lie. When I was three or four—my first memories, brief images, sensations—I'd been overcome by violent bouts of desire when I looked at the boys in the playground, fully aware that this was what already separated me from my family, what made my relationship with you impossible and skewed. When I looked at the boys at school I'd have liked to feel their skin on mine, the warmth of their hands on my face. As I grew up I silently longed for the men around me, those I saw sawing wood in their gardens in preparation for winter, their muscles taut as they operated the chainsaw or carried logs two by two and stacked them in the shed, the men I went to watch at football matches every Sunday. I'd look at their legs and the outline of their cocks under the fabric of their shorts as they ran around the field and I'd have liked them to press my face against their thighs.

Can parents imagine images like this populating their children's imaginations? Could you have imagined such turmoil behind my childish mask?

When I saw the men gathered at the café, often truck drivers because it was one of the few jobs still available in the village since the factories had closed down, and one of them gave me a lift in his truck, I felt his breath waft over to me from his seat and prayed that he'd stop on a lonely road between the forests and the ponds and ask me to touch his body. A man had done that with my sister. He'd given her a lift in his truck and asked her to touch his cock through his jeans and I'd dreamed of this scene every day, several times a day. I didn't understand why my sister had been so lucky and not me. She'd come home in tears. She told my brother, who said he'd get the guy for what he'd done, and when I heard her crying I didn't understand, I loathed her for her ingratitude, I didn't understand how the scene I hoped for more than anything and which defined the very contours of my fantasies and obsessions could make her sad, while I'd have given anything to be in her place.

This secret contaminated my entire childhood.

Although I was bursting with desire, shame made me hate anything that could remind me of who I was. I was afraid of myself. One evening the lycée took us to see a play called

Angels in America at the Maison de la Culture. I'd never heard of it. Gérard, our drama teacher, had told us it was about homosexuality and like every time I'd heard that word since the first day of my life my heart beat faster in my chest. I'd looked around, hoping that this tension in my body wasn't visible to the others, it was always the same sensation, every time the word homosexuality was mentioned my pulse would race because I was sure that someone just had to say it and everyone would see that it had to do with me. I'd got very skillful at deflecting the conversation; when someone brought up homosexuality I always found an urgent topic to divert everyone's attention, Did you see the attack in the States, Did you see who died, What're we doing tonight (and the flush on my cheeks, on my face).

I sat down next to Elena in the auditorium of the big theater and the show started. No sooner had the first minutes gone by than men were kissing, undressing, making love to each other; I'd never seen such a direct, explicit representation of homosexuality, and so of my own desire, of my secret— and, I think I can say, of my being. I stood up in the middle of the play and said, *I don't want to see this homo crap it disgusts me.* Elena was surprised, and when they came out some of the other girls told me that I was stupid and homophobic. Their insults reassured me. What these girls, Chloé, Sophie and even Elena, didn't know was that once I was out of the auditorium I cried because of what I'd seen, I cried out of self-hatred. I cried because I knew that more than anything else I'd have loved to watch that play right through to the end.

I don't know what triggered it, if there was a scene, an image or an apparition, but one night when Cynthia had gone to her father's place and I was alone in the flat I decided to go online to do what I'd always dreamed of doing; I wanted to try to meet someone, a man. I'd waited too long, lied too much, and that night I promised myself that all of that was over; I got up from the sofa and my decision echoed in my body; I thought: *you're gay*, the phrase pulsed in my skull— the word gay seemed so foreign, so violent, almost grotesque in its sound and simplicity, it could not contain within it all the complexity of what I'd felt since birth, my desire, my fear, my hope, my shame, my secrecy—it hurt me and fascinated me at the same time, I'd repeated it thousands of times in my head over the past weeks, gay, gay, gay, gay, as if by repeating it I could discover something about myself, I repeated it and the pain increased—I don't mean an abstract pain like when people say "words that hurt," but real pain, with all my joints and bones pulling at each other, my whole body was trembling, I was cold; I walked the few steps to my computer and I swear those were the hardest steps of my life; my legs resisted, they gelled, my body rebelled against my decision. I wanted to walk but my muscles wouldn't obey, they wanted to stop me. I sat down at the computer, turned it on, tried to catch my breath and wrote in the search bar "Meet gay man," I remember, those exact words. I looked around the living room as if someone might have seen me, my fingers were damp, my forehead was damp, and my body was still cold and trembling. It was spring outside but the cold came from within me, from my rib cage. How could three such simple words have been so difficult to write, why had it taken me seventeen years to dare to do something so banal, so trivial as typing those words on a keyboard? I couldn't bring myself to press the "enter" key to start the search, I couldn't breathe, I was going to die, here, in this living room, I was going to die, I wanted to die, I was afraid I was going to die, I was suffocating. I took a deep breath and continued. I let two, three seconds pass, I thought Count to three, and I pressed the key. Dozens of websites appeared, chatting and dating forums, I didn't know which one to choose; I clicked on a random link. You had to register, give an email address and a pseudonym to be able to chat with other men on the site. I opened another window to create a new email address, a different one from the one I used the rest of the time to communicate with Elena or the Maison de la Culture, I couldn't risk opening my emails in front of people I knew in Amiens and receiving messages from this site—I was afraid, it was fear that made me cold, before that night I had no idea that feelings had a temperature of their own. I went back to the forum page and created a profile. I didn't put my real name. I wrote a few lines to describe myself, something like Romain, young, 17, looking for my first date with a man, and I couldn't believe I was writing such bold words. I wanted to backpedal, turn off the computer and go back to living like I did before, *you don't need this, you've managed to live in secrecy all these years*, I knew, I was aware that if I met a man my whole life would change—but I kept going, I remained in front of the screen. Within seconds I received messages from dozens of men, most of them asking me how I was doing, others sending me pictures of their cock.

I answered a few but I had to stop; suddenly my gut wrenched; something was shifting inside me; I felt soiled by what I was doing, my whole past was waking up inside me, all of the insults at school, the things people in the village said against homosexuality, it had all been engraved in me and this collective disgust was trying to stop me now, the self of my desire and the self of my past were going head to head in my body, I felt like the most revolting thing in the world, a fag, a fairy, a homo, a pansy, a poof, the worst thing in the world, a metaphor for filth and dishonor.

I got up, ran to the toilet and threw up. My body was imploding. I crouched on the floor and bent my head over the toilet bowl. All of my muscles were aching, not breathing but wheezing I knelt on the floor, I was an animal, my hands clinging to the toilet, my face over the gunky, stinking water.

I was suffering but it was too late, I couldn't stop. I rinsed my mouth and went back to the computer, and with trembling hands I continued writing to strangers.

There was one man I chatted with a little more than the rest. His name was Pierre. He seemed more sensitive, more patient than the others. I trembled but I answered his questions. I told him that my real name wasn't Romain but Eddy—I didn't dare to say Édouard, I didn't yet feel comfortable enough to use my chosen name outside of my close circle of friends. I chatted with him until late in the night and he said we could meet up the following week if I liked.

I said okay.

My whole life was turning upside down.

I MET PIERRE. HE CAME TO SEE ME IN THE FLAT ON BOU-
levard Carnot and we made love. I remember every detail, the
sun outside, the warm breath of air coming through the open
window, my first glimpse of him when he parked, the sharp,
brutal thunk of the car door as it closed. When he entered
the flat and I kissed him I thought, *I'm kissing a man*, the
phrase echoed as my lips touched his. Every ounce of him was
a synonym for the word Freedom, Freedom from you, from
my whole life, Freedom the beard on his face, Freedom the
muscles under the fabric of his T-shirt, Freedom the hair on
his arms, Freedom his cock stiffening under his jeans, Freedom from what the world wanted of me.

I don't think it's normal, I don't know, but when he lay
naked on top of me, it was you I thought of (in telling you
this I'm saying the unspeakable). To have a naked man against
my body, his cock pressed against my skin, was to go beyond
the limits of what you considered the most base, the most

vile. To do what I was doing was to enter a reality that was
radically opposed to the social class of my childhood, to the
village, it was to break definitively with the milieu I'd shared
with you and its hatred and disgust at the mere idea of such a
thing. Making love with a man and letting him penetrate me
resulted from the same will, the same process, as going to the
cinema and learning to speak without a northern accent, that
of escaping from the past.

In making love with a man I rejected all the values of my
milieu, I became bourgeois.

*   *   *

On a sheet of paper I'd written: *Desire is opening the doors of the
world to me.* Pierre spent the night and I saw him again. When
he couldn't come to Amiens I took the train to the small town
in the Paris suburbs where he lived. Through him I discovered
yet another life, his friends, the colleagues he invited to eat
with us in the evening, people whose nearness to Paris set
them apart from those I knew in Amiens. Everything revolved
around tiny nuances, the way they dressed, what they talked
about and the things they ate, minute details and facts, it's in-
credible how the world can take refuge in the smallest things,
the fact that they drank sparkling water rather than still water
at dinner, the way they talked about politics in a more personal
tone, as if they thrived on their proximity to their politicians,
whereas in Amiens the world of political power was perceived
as distant, inaccessible, and also something a little like arrogance, their certainty of their place in the world. I sensed

that his friends' geographical characteristics, the fact that they lived so close to the capital, had a direct bearing on how they felt and acted (this feeling will be confirmed later on when I go to Paris and see how different people's bodies are there, not just because of their proximity to the capital but also because of their presence and immersion in it, their being at its heart, as if it was enough to place a body in a geographically different setting to change it completely, as if bodies were above all, or at least in part, geographical in nature).

I didn't tell Elena or anyone else about my other life. I was living two lives: one that was articulated in language in my day-to-day conversations, and the other silent, secret one inside me. When I spoke with my friends in Amiens or with Lucas and Satine, my co-workers at the theater, I thought of my other life, my secret journeys to the suburbs of Paris, and I felt like I was more alive than they were, my secret life combined with my visible life made my existence deeper, denser.

My affair with Pierre couldn't last. I'd lost too many years of desire and wanted to meet other men. I went online as I'd done to meet him. A big hotel had just opened in the city center opposite the cathedral and a lot of the men showing up on the dating websites would ask me to come and visit them in their room; I'd go, several times a week, at night so as not to be seen. I'd walk past the reception and head straight for the lifts as if I were a guest, I tried to walk toward them—the lifts—with a confident gait and enough arrogance on my face so that the person on the night shift would think it out of place, stretching the bounds of politeness, to request information from someone as distinguished as me. I braced my legs and raised my chin and went up to join the man I'd just been chatting with online. *(I can't put the images of my years in the village and those nights in the hotel side by side, it's as if it was impossible for them to belong to the same being, as if the story of my life wasn't the story of one person through time but a succession of characters who have nothing to do with each other, who don't even share a name.)* There were men staying at the hotel who'd come in from Germany, the Netherlands, England, or who'd just returned from Asia or the United States. After we'd made love, in the darkened room, they told me of their lives as I rested my head on their chest, my body warm and moist.

I listened to them and it was as if the contact with them gave me a heightened degree of reality, as if by listening to them and making love with them I continued my escape, venturing deeper and deeper into the world, the child I'd been could never have imagined that one day he'd meet strangers in the night and that each evening they'd describe to him their life in another country—Gilles Deleuze says somewhere that when you meet someone it's a landscape, and not a person, you fall in love with, a landscape with its own scenery, its own geography, its own features, and every night I discovered one landscape more.

I TOLD ELENA EVERYTHING. I COULDN'T LEAD HER ON anymore. I sat down at the computer and wrote her a long message telling her about it all, the desire I'd hidden since childhood, the faked relationships with girls at the lycée to avoid suspicion, my affair with Pierre. I was afraid as I wrote to her. She told me that it didn't change anything, that she loved me—or rather, she didn't say it didn't change anything, as people often awkwardly do and as other friends would do later when I told them the same thing, but she did ask me questions, she wanted to understand what the secrecy, silence, suffering and shame had meant for me. She encouraged me. She took me to the cinema to see films about homosexuality, she told me about the authors who'd written about men who desired other men—and I, who never read, read *Death in Venice* in one night, in the guest room next to Elena's, trembling, shaken by the realization that there was a whole history of books dedicated to the desires, the beauty, the suffering and the lives of people like me.

She'd come to my place for dinner, we listened to Ella Fitzgerald or Debussy records and went for walks in the afternoon, I remember we spent a whole day in a big luxury department store where she put on one hat after another and I tried on ties and cravats. We drank tea in a chic, almost completely silent salon where a woman offered us a dozen different brews, and we prepared for our exams together. Elena had told me I shouldn't be afraid to go to the city's gay bar, Le Red and White, and I went. There I met someone, Nicolas, he had money, he took me to the Paris Opera, he had paintings on the wall of his living room and made me feel *different*. When I didn't want to stay in the flat on Boulevard Carnot because Cynthia was there, I stayed with Nicolas or Alice, a friend from the lycée who lived in a huge house behind the cathedral. Her father was an important doctor, they too changed the tenor of my life, Alice organized screenings of Antonioni films in her garden, she did theater, made jewelry. I was so far removed from my past. My work at the Maison de la Culture was going well, I felt liked by the others. I was going to university, my results were fine, I hardly saw Mom, my brothers and sisters or you, for me that was no big deal, I didn't miss you. I spent my days and evenings with Elena, sometimes with other friends, Julie, Étienne or Alice, we talked about films by Alfred Hitchcock or Pedro Almodóvar, admired photos by Nan Goldin or Robert Doisneau on my computer, and acted out scenes from Shakespeare or Jean-Luc Lagarce in my little living room. What I'm trying to tell you is that I was entirely bound up with life in Amiens, even more so and more naturally since I'd stopped hiding things from Elena. And it was exactly at that moment, when I felt completely integrated, that I met Didier, and that I resolved to start all over and run away again.

II

DIDIER

(breakup)

IMPACT

HOW COULD I HAVE GUESSED THAT ONE DAY AMIENS would become what the village had been just a few years earlier, a place I'd have to flee? That one day I'd understand that in fact being in Amiens meant remaining a prisoner of my childhood, and if I wanted to take my revenge on my past I'd have to escape from this town just as I'd escaped from the village?

Everything started as dozens of other days had started: Elena had asked me to go with her to the university to hear a philosopher speak about his latest book. I'd been to such lectures with her in the past, and on the rare occasions when I still talked to my mother on the phone and she asked me what I'd done that week, I'd say *I went to a guest lecture.* Saying that gave me a sense of pride and superiority that now makes me cringe, because she didn't know what a guest lecture was and I saw in this gap a sign of my distance and success. Elena had told me that this lecture wouldn't be like the others because the philosopher who was coming to speak had written a book about his own life, called *Returning to Reims*. In it he explained that he'd been born into a working-class family in northern France; later he'd become a world-renowned author and intellectual, and he'd used his own path in life, his passage from one extremity of the world to the other, as a way of reflecting on poverty, domination and class violence. His book wasn't like other scholarly works, Elena told me with a smile.

I sat down next to her* in the front row to hear the philosopher speak. I'd bought his book that afternoon in the hope of having him sign it, and was holding it in my hands. I looked at Elena, her black hair, her smile. She was the only one in that hot, humid, crowded room who knew that I hadn't just come to hear him talk about poverty, self-transformation and social classes, but also about homosexuality; Elena had told me that it was homosexuality that had made him flee to Paris and reinvent himself as an intellectual, that his sexuality had been the instrument of his freedom, and that was what his book was about.

The philosopher started to speak. All around me I saw people grabbing their pens and scribbling down what he said; I was fascinated by how important his words were to them.

---

* In fact I didn't go to the lecture with Elena but with another friend—the same guy I'd imitated when I enrolled in the history department at the university. I prefer to substitute Elena for him in this story, for the sake of coherence and above all so as not to have to retrace the whole series of events that led me to go with him and not with her. Anyway, I told Elena every detail, and it was as if she'd been present the whole time, even when she wasn't.

He talked about how his homosexuality had distanced him from his family and the world around him from his earliest childhood onward (*and I thought to myself: like me*). He explained how he'd had to run away, and how movement in an immobile world had allowed him to see reality differently (*and I thought: like me*). He described his first homosexual experiences, the men he met in secret behind the cathedral in his hometown, at night, and above all the way of being in the world and seeing the world that he'd invented for himself as a result of his homosexuality. He cited names I'd never heard, Oscar Wilde, Violette Leduc, Jean Genet, Monique Wittig. I sat there in the front row, listening to him talk.

I felt something rising up inside me, but I didn't yet know what it was.

He went on to describe the impossibility of speaking with his own family because of his transformation, and the sense of remoteness he felt. He explained how at twenty he'd left for Paris, the capital, the big city where everything seemed possible, to study philosophy and live more freely than he had in Reims, his hometown. He said that in Paris he began to write books and invent himself as an intellectual. My heart stirred in my chest. Everything was changing around me. Now I understood what I'd felt as soon as he started to speak: Why hadn't I done what he'd done? Why wasn't I like him? Why hadn't I gone to Paris—like him? Why had I been so timid in escaping from the past? His words propelled my body far from the room where I was sitting; all at once I was far from the others, and—for the first time—from Elena as well.

I listened to him, he spoke, I listened, and suddenly I thought, *I'd like to be like him, I'd like to be him*—why didn't I run away as far as he did? I no longer knew what I felt, I envied him, I was fascinated and the next moment my feelings switched to a blend of jealousy and anger, *Why did he succeed while I'm still here, stuck in this small provincial town where I've hardly read a thing, I've written nothing but a few worthless dramatic sketches plagiarized from Elena, why him and not me—* I wanted to tune him out, I wanted him to shut up, *shut him up, please*—I was infuriated at him for having what I didn't have, and then my emotions switched again and I thought I'd never admired anyone with so much force; I turned to Elena and saw her body drifting away. I couldn't touch her anymore, I wanted to call out to her but she wouldn't hear me. When the philosopher finished his talk—his name was Didier Eribon, I didn't know it yet but soon I'd simply call him Didier, soon he'd be my friend, he'd replace Elena in my life and without meaning to he'd bring about the most heart-wrenching break-up I would ever experience—I went over to where he was sitting to ask him to sign my copy of his book. Other people were waiting too, I let them go first, I wanted to be able to talk to him, I wanted the others to leave so I could be alone with him and tell him that I was like him, I needed to, I don't know why it mattered so much to me, *I have to tell him that I'm like him, I have to tell him that I also left, that I was also separated from the world of my childhood by my desire, my secret, I have to tell him that I also*—I was thinking too much, too fast, my mouth was drying up. I took a few steps toward the table where he was signing books and handed him my copy; I couldn't speak, I was afraid I'd say something that would make me look silly in his eyes. I stammered, I'm like you, I really liked what you said tonight. I looked down and thought, *Now it's over. He thinks you're an idiot. He thinks you're an idiot and he'll never be interested in anyone like you.* I bit my tongue to punish myself for what I'd said; he smiled and said thank you, and added that the people who'd organized the event had invited him for a drink afterward and that I could join them if I liked, the bar they were going to was just down the street—it was a bar I knew, I'd been there with Elena. I couldn't believe my ears. Why had he asked me and not the others? (Later he'd tell me that my eyes and my attitude had betrayed how ardently I meant what I'd said.) I followed the group to the bar where several tables had been reserved and sat near him so we could talk. I told him my name was Eddy; as with Pierre I didn't dare say Édouard. I repeated—*I had to repeat it*, maybe I did it for myself, maybe it was a way of reassuring myself, of telling myself that I wasn't alone—that my sufferings and desires resembled other sufferings and desires, I told him that my story resembled his, or rather that I would like it to resemble his, and he answered with a smile: *So do it, transform your life.* He talked to me, I talked to him, I tried to show him that I was worth looking at and listening to, that I was worthy of him.

It took something as simple, as circumstantial as a guest lecture for my fate to change completely and irreversibly.

Something was happening inside me as I walked back at the end of the evening with Elena, something violent and unprecedented, my thoughts resumed *Why haven't I left?* Everything

Didier had said revived the pain, the bitter taste of the insults in my mouth, the pain of exclusion in the village, my father's shame because my voice was too high, the way he lowered his eyes in embarrassment when I spoke in front of other people, all of this came back and I saw that I hadn't escaped it, that my simply being in Amiens meant that I was still attached to my past and all that went with it. It's true, *why hadn't it occurred to me before*, I knew people who'd grown up in the village and now lived in Amiens, people who like me had left to come to *the big provincial town*, it was rare but not completely unheard of, I hadn't escaped a thing. That evening, through the meeting with Didier and everything it made possible, I understood that my revenge had only just begun. If I really wanted to avenge the child I'd been, like Didier I had to go to Paris and do what he'd done: write books and gain worldwide recognition, that was what I said to myself. Hadn't the child I'd been dreamed of speaking in front of audiences sitting in rapt attention—like Didier? Hadn't I promised myself that one day I'd be famous and important, hadn't I wanted the boys at school to see what I'd become and pay for what they'd done to me, to regret their acts and suffer from the gap between their lives and mine? Hadn't I spent years as a child interviewing myself in front of the mirror in the morning to feel like I existed? Hadn't I spent all the early years of my life watching people on television and dreaming of becoming visible in turn?

I always talk too much, I have too many stories to tell, I have to tell this one: one day I was playing football in the village with three other boys, Kevin, Dimitri and Steven, I was twelve, Kevin had kicked the ball too hard and sent it flying out of the empty lot where we were playing and into the garden of an old woman we called the Witch. No one had the guts to go and get it, everyone was afraid of the Witch, so Kevin said to me, Eddy, if you go I swear we'll never call you a queer or a homo again. Suddenly I dreamed of a new life free of insults. I said okay and ran over to the Witch's garden, faster than I'd ever run, I climbed the barbed-wire fence although I was normally so scared of barbed wire, usually I crawled under barbed wire when Kevin or Steven climbed over it, they jumped over and I crawled under, but this time I did it, I jumped over it, I was no longer afraid of the Witch, I came back and handed the ball to Kevin, I'd done what no one else had dared to do, I could already see my new life without insults, I believed it, but when Kevin took the ball he said Thank you, Miss Poof. The others fell about laughing, they laughed so hard they had to kneel on the grass to catch their breath. After the evening with the philosopher it was this pain that reawoke in me because I realized that I hadn't managed to get as far from it as I'd thought. I was in so much pain.

Elena asked me if I'd enjoyed the evening and I thought *How could I have been wrong for so long, for so many years?* I said *Yes*, but it was just a way of stopping the conversation, preventing it from happening, of not talking, of not being there, I was no longer there, in that street in Amiens, my body was just going through the motions, and I thought *For all these years I was sure I'd changed and become someone else but I was wrong. I thought I'd run away but I was a prisoner in this city, this city trapped me, it lied to me, it made me believe it was a place where I could be free but it was anything but, it was all a lie, I was living a lie.* I looked around me and the streets that had seemed immense and limitless the whole time I'd been in Amiens were tiny now, they were closing in on me, I looked around me, *I want to leave, I want out.*

I remembered that the very first time I came to Amiens it had taken me more than two hours to get from the station to the lycée, even though they were less than half a mile apart, because I got lost, the city seemed so vast. Now I thought *I hate this city, I have to leave.* Elena's look changed. She could tell something was wrong. *Are you sure you're all right?* and I said *Yes, yes,* but my Yes didn't mean Yes, my Yes meant *Stop talking.* Now all I could hear were the words in my head: *I have to get out of here, I have to leave.*

NOW IT COMES BACK TO ME, ELENA USED TO LAUGH AND say that my teeth and jaw were so deformed that the day I died she'd take my skull and use it as an ashtray. She was the only one who could say things like that without hurting me.

I'D JOINED THE HAIKU CLUB AT THE LYCÉE WITH HER. WE wrote erotic haikus that couldn't be hung on the library walls along with the others because of their subject matter. I think she must have laughed about that for at least a year. And I laughed with her.

SHE ALWAYS FINISHED HER LUNCH BEFORE I DID AND when she had nothing left on her plate she'd start eating from mine. When I protested she'd say "I haven't eaten for two days!" and I'd shrug.

THE NEXT DAY

THE DAY AFTER THE LECTURE I WOKE UP EXHAUSTED, I hadn't slept. I'd spent the night dreaming about my life far from Amiens, both discouraged by the journey that lay ahead and flushed with hope during the brief moments when I thought it was possible, that I was going to do it. I imagined posters in the streets announcing talks I'd give, like Didier, with my name printed all over town and the shame of my childhood forever erased. I imagined myself as a famous writer.

I want to be clear: for me the key thing was change and liberation, not books or writing. I don't think my primary obsession was with books. If I suddenly dreamed of becoming a writer, it wasn't writing I dreamed of but extracting myself from my past once and for all, and that opportunity presented itself when I met Didier, that's all. What I'm writing shouldn't be seen as the story of the birth of a writer but as the birth of freedom, of being uprooted at all costs from a hated past. And if I'd met a dancer from the Paris Opera Ballet or the Bolshoi who'd come to present his work rather than an author like Didier, and if it were still possible, would I have wanted to escape from Amiens by becoming a dancer rather than an author, would I have put all my energy and strength into making that happen, the way I wanted to imitate Didier by becoming an intellectual? I think so. I think I wanted to change in order to free myself, and I would have taken any path that presented itself to escape. It's just that this way out—writing books—was the one that presented itself to me, through the encounter with Elena and then hearing Didier speak; books and writing offered me the only real, concrete possibility of changing once again.

When I woke up I walked over to the shower and there too I thought, *I've got to change.* I left the flat and outside I unfolded the crumpled piece of paper in my pocket on which I'd jotted down the titles of the books Didier had mentioned during his talk the day before. I walked to the bookshop; I'd taken the money I'd saved over the past two years working at the Maison de la Culture and I bought around ten books, Pierre Bourdieu, James Baldwin, Émile Durkheim, Marguerite Duras, Erving Goffman, Jacques Derrida, Assia Djebar, Patrick Chamoiseau, Simone de Beauvoir. I knew that if I wanted to write I had to read, I couldn't wait, I was already too far behind, I was seventeen and had hardly read a thing. I went home promising myself that I'd read all the books I'd just bought in the days that followed, even though despite my transformation with Elena over the past years I'd mostly talked about books without reading them, because until now this illusion had sufficed.

TRANSITION

THE INSOMNIA AFTER THE CONFERENCE. I IMAGINED Nadya taking stock of my metamorphosis, seeing that I was transformed, famous, like Didier, and saying to her friends *You know when he arrived in Amiens he was nothing, he fought hard to come this far.*

The admiration she inspired in her listeners overwhelmed me.

* * *

Then came the first time when I explained to Elena that I couldn't go to the cinema with her when she came to pick me up, saying that I had to stay home and read. It was the first time I'd said something like that. She'd known me for four years and I'd never said anything like it.

She looked at me as if she was trying to decipher my face, and unmask someone who'd usurped my body and identity. She shrugged, What are you reading? I showed her the cover,

Distinction: A Social Critique of the Judgement of Taste. She'd never heard of it. The scene of our encounter was reversed, this time I was the one who was reading and she was the one who didn't know the book (but I wasn't happy about it, I was afraid to grow apart from her).

*   *   *

I read, but I didn't understand what I was reading, the sentences were too complex, the books referred to notions and concepts I was unfamiliar with and couldn't grasp. I kept at it, telling myself that I'd understand later after I'd finished reading, that each book would give me the keys I needed to understand the one I'd read the day before, I tried to persuade myself that if I understood one page in fifty I'd already have accomplished a lot—I couldn't always convince myself—or lie to myself—and some evenings I'd get discouraged by the pages of an open book, unable to decipher a simple succession of letters and words, I hated myself, I despised myself, *I'll never make it.* I labored to find a way into books that resisted, as if the sentences were physically pushing me away. I suffered for being myself. But I kept reading, I thought: If you don't become an author you'll have lost everything. After several hours of reading I tried to write short texts; I practiced, and didn't show anyone what I'd done. I know what I'm saying may seem odd, it's hard to imagine someone who's never read and never really written anything suddenly devoting all his time, all his madness, all his energy to doing just that, but that's how it was.

*   *   *

More images.

*   *   *

The time when I was twelve, during a walk organized by the village sports association, I started comparing the people walking with me to characters in my favorite TV series. There were around ten of us on a dirt road, surrounded by miles of fields and forests. I pointed to each one in turn, You're like Rebecca, you're more like Michael, and you're Laetitia. There was a gay character in the series, an effeminate guy who everyone made jokes about. His name was Thomas. When I said to my aunt And I don't know who you are, she replied You may not know who I am, Eddy, but you, you're Thomas. Everyone walking with us laughed, Yes of course, Thomas the fruitcake.

I wanted to die.

*   *   *

The times at school when my father asked me to tell the accountant that we couldn't pay the canteen fees, my shame when he replied Surely your parents can pay that. It's not a lot, tell them to make an effort.

*   *   *

When a boy at the lycée said to me My underwear costs as much as your whole wardrobe.

*   *   *

The time when I was fourteen, just after I met Elena, when I was still going back to the village and Kevin invited me to a barbecue in the empty lot behind his house. It was summer, and hot. Kevin lit the fire when night fell, we drank whisky with orange juice and ate grilled meat, sitting around the flames, a dozen or so of us. We were laughing, and suddenly Kevin's father, who was there with us and who'd drunk too much, said So, Eddy, it seems you like cock. Is it true, is that what spins your crank? Sucking a big fat knob? The others laughed, and I pretended to laugh too. The more he insulted me the more I laughed, a taste of steel and blood in my mouth.

* * *

All the times at school when I didn't have the money for an afternoon snack, unlike the children from wealthier families who had biscuits in shiny red, green and blue wrappers, those times when at the age of ten or eleven I already understood the meaning of the word class.

* * *

The day during an argument with my little brother when he said to me in my mother's presence, Anyway everyone in the village says you're a queer. I was terrified that she'd heard him. I ran out of the house and stayed in the fields until past midnight. I didn't want to come home and see my mother's questioning eyes, Is it true what your little brother said?

* * *

Reading those books, becoming like Didier, leaving Amiens, was a way of distancing myself from all of these images. Of beating them. Meeting Didier revived my childhood, it brought it back to me and because of that I had to escape it again.

*   *   *

The philosopher Eve Kosofsky Sedgwick speaks somewhere of the inexhaustible transformative energy a stigmatized childhood can produce.

*   *   *

I had to go on.

*   *   *

And then the memories of victories, reawakened after the meeting with Didier.

*   *   *

The day when, at twelve, I'd written a little play for the school, not really a play but more like a few comic scenes, to celebrate the end of the year, that we performed in front of all the students and teachers, at the end of which everyone stood up to applaud me, several hundred people, and I thought Now no one will dare to insult me, I've won, you've won.

*   *   *

That other day when Madame Roger, my history teacher at the lycée, said with a smile in her voice Mr. Bellegueule, you are simply exceptional.

* * *

The year at the lycée when I was selected out of the whole drama class to appear in a film with the actress Isabelle Huppert. The others only dreamed about it.

* * *

If I wrote a book I'd get that same feeling, only multiplied by ten. I'd prove to the world that I was a somebody and that it had been wrong to want to put me down.

* * *

I had to read, read as much as I could.

* * *

Oh and I'm forgetting the turning point, when after several weeks I started having a better grasp of what I was reading, when the fits and tears became less and less frequent, and when every idea in one book reminded me of other ideas in other books. I was experiencing the first results of my work and effort. During the evenings I spent with Elena, Julie and my other friends in Amiens, my conversation was bolstered by everything I knew, everything I'd just learned, and I sensed their admiration.

I understood that Knowledge = Power.

* * *

In the evenings at the Maison de la Culture I'd show people to their seats, and then more and more often once the show had started I'd sit outside and read. The rule was that two ushers had to sit at the front doors while the others sat inside the theater, and I asked Léa and the rest if I could be outside as much as possible; I think they were surprised by my sudden, almost total transformation. They'd see me coming in every day with a different book, Hannah Arendt, Martin Heidegger, Gilles Deleuze, I'd read at work and at night as well, I'd read during lunch at the university, I'd read on the bus, always with the same thought: *I have to leave, I have to leave. I have to change.*

* * *

I no longer liked Amiens.

* * *

There was Elena, but I was sure she'd come with me to Paris.

* * *

Or rather: I think I knew she wouldn't come, but I made myself believe she would so I wouldn't have to face what I was doing: preparing to abandon her.

So I'd be pleased, happy even . . .
. . . to discuss all these questions with you (you're such
pleasant company!)
On the bus when you said we might have dinner
together, I felt the elation well up inside me.
I'd wanted to suggest it but didn't dare.

So is it still on? Would you like to have dinner in town
while you're in Amiens for your seminar?

I await your answer not without a certain impatience,
and wish you an enjoyable weekend.

* * *

I'd been thinking about it for several days. I was going to
write to Didier and ask him to go out for a drink. I sat down
at my computer and typed *Dear Didier Eribon*. I looked at
those three words, I could hear my heart beating, I could
feel my lungs in my throat, I reread them, *Dear Didier Eribon*, but I couldn't go on, I was too afraid he'd say no and
put me in my place. I couldn't write anything else, I couldn't
think of a single sentence, I wanted to express feelings and no
sentence could translate them without betraying them. The
tension in my body stood for everything, my story, my past,
my childhood, my dreams, and it wanted nothing to do with
words (and I thought: *Maybe I should dance. Maybe moving my
muscles can show my feelings better than words*). I waited, for a
long time, and then my body gave way and the words came.
I started again, *Dear Didier Eribon*. I told him that my story

and my past were the same as his, that I recognized myself in him, that I wanted to become like him, I no longer knew, was I him or did I want to become him. The email ended with an invitation maybe to have dinner with me, a shy request, *Is it still on? Would you like to have dinner?*

He accepted. He said he'd be pleased to have a drink with me and maybe even dinner. I got his email and ran straight to Elena's house, oblivious to everything around me. When I got to her place I whooped: *He accepted, he said yes, he even said we could have dinner together, can you believe it?* She smiled. I didn't see how bitter she was. I was too selfish, I wanted to leave. I didn't yet understand—unlike her, who always saw things sooner and clearer than I did—that what I'd come to announce was the beginning of our separation.

*   *   *

In his reply Didier told me that he was teaching at the University of Amiens; it was only then that I found out that even before I met him he'd been close to me, in the same town, and I hadn't known it. I asked him for permission to go to all his lectures, including the ones he gave to graduate and doctoral students, and he replied that I was welcome to attend. I didn't want to miss a single one, I was sure that by sitting in on them I'd learn things that would accelerate my metamorphosis. During the months that followed his first lecture, between the time I decided to leave for Paris and my departure, I sat in the front row of all his classes, without exception, I wrote down the titles of the books he mentioned, I bought them and read them. I imitated Didier, his way of speaking, his way of looking and smiling. I talked about him and his books to Elena and my other friends in Amiens, Alice, Julie and Juliette, a new friend I'd met at the university, and when I did I made it sound as if we were closer than we were.

*   *   *

Was I becoming a bad person? Was I repeating in Amiens the violence I'd done to my family a few years earlier, when I'd go back to my mother's place and pretend to be reading on the sofa to show her who I was becoming? In changing, did I want others to understand that I was no longer like them, had I understood that changing didn't only mean becoming someone else but also *no longer being like other people*, and so rejecting those people, abandoning them, putting them hopelessly below myself? Had I become hateful?

I no longer went out to bars on the nights I wasn't working in the theater.

Since I'd arrived in Amiens, when Elena stayed in with her parents I usually went out to bars with other friends, spent the night drinking vodka with them and came home drunk and barely able to walk at four or five in the morning. I remember singing with them, our voices in the night, before the meeting with Didier hurled me headlong into the future, before the future and the hope of the future completely invaded my existence, before the present all but disappeared from my life. And in fact after I met Didier, when Julie or Étienne would come to pick me up, I'd tell them that I couldn't go out, that I had work to do, that I had to stay home and read one of the books Didier had mentioned in class. The first couple of times they looked at me with the same astonishment as Elena, but when the scene repeated itself their astonishment turned into a form of hostility, until one evening when Étienne looked at me and said *Now he thinks he's Mr. Bigshot, what's got into him? Ever since he went to that guy's lecture he's been acting like a Parisian.*

His words hurt me.

I didn't know my dream was so visible.

PARIS, THE FIRST TIMES

SINCE I'D BEEN ATTENDING DIDIER'S LECTURES AND since our first drink together, I'd been seeing him once a week. I told him about my plans to write books and move to Paris— basically to imitate what he'd done at about my age and described in his guest lecture. He invited me to a restaurant one evening, it was a Tuesday, and that first invitation turned into a sort of ritual, I'd meet him every Tuesday in the same restaurant, we were growing closer. I'd never been to a restaurant before, except on one or two special occasions, and when I sat down at the table he'd reserved I was intoxicated by the sensation of being served—as if I was living a life that wasn't my own and the pleasure that flowed through me was that of a thief. On those evenings he'd take me into a world different from anything I'd ever known, with stories about his friends who were writers, philosophers and artists, accounts of his days writing and correcting his manuscripts and of the gay life in Paris, going to gay bars and spending time with a community of friends whose sexuality, and the complicity based on it, he shared. He was friends with authors that Elena admired, they were part of his private life, he called them by their first names. I felt a sense of urgency surge through my body: I couldn't wait, I wanted to go to Paris as soon as I could. Not only was I keen to live my new life and as fast as possible, I also knew that in Paris I'd be able to meet men, and my desire was occupying more and more space inside me since the steps I'd taken with Pierre. I told Didier and he encouraged me. He said that in Paris I'd meet wonderful people, that I'd experience a freedom I'd never known, and after this conversation with him I decided to go there every weekend.

The first times in Paris it was like I was exploring a totally new life, stronger and more beautiful than the one I'd known. I met people who led lives I could never have imagined, and who made me dream: students at the Academy of Dramatic Arts who staged performances in seedy bars, artists who didn't have the career they'd have liked and who gave theater or dance lessons in neighborhood associations—but even what they considered failures and rejections were for me signs of freedom and a bohemian lifestyle. Life in Amiens seemed hemmed in by comparison; I wanted to have their life. In the bars I went to I met lawyers, journalists, architects—professions that in Paris seemed to hold infinite privileges, lives of wealth, independence, importance, and trips around the world. With these people I put into practice what I'd learned from Elena, cultural references, ways of eating and speaking. *(Is this what Nadya would mean years later when she said I took advantage of everything she gave me?)*

I'd walk for entire days discovering the city, six, seven hours of walking without stopping, I'd drink a hot chocolate or a tomato juice in a café for lunch; I was happy. I delved into Sim-

one de Beauvoir's memoirs, which Didier had recommended
to me, and I wanted to live the same life as her, an intellectual
life; I'd read on café terraces, I'd meet up with Didier in the
brasseries of Montparnasse and he'd tell me about the manuscript he was working on, the talks he was giving or the col-
loquiums he was taking part in, he'd say things directly linked
to his life as an author, "I have to write my lecture for next
week," "I have to answer my editor," and I dreamed of being
able to say such things myself. One afternoon he invited me to
go to the opera with him and I was dumbstruck, I don't know
if it was the beauty of the music or if being at the opera made
me feel like I was truly bourgeois, no doubt there's no distin-
guishing between the two. What image could have been more
diametrically opposed to my father than me sitting beside an
author in the Paris Opera House?

You must have experienced it to understand it, neverthe-
less I will try to explain, everything I did had a dizzying sig-
nificance because the whole history of the world, with all its
lapses and injustices, infused every aspect of my life. I'd go
into the opera house and think I should never have come here,
I'd sit on the terrace of a café in the Marais district to read a
book by Derrida or Arendt and think I shouldn't be here at
all, I shouldn't know these authors existed. I felt a kind of pity,
or at least sadness, for those who went to grand Parisian the-
aters or sat on the terrace of a café without understanding how
lucky they were, without awe, who performed those gestures
as they'd performed them in their childhood, as their parents
and grandparents had performed them before them, because
they'd been born into a more privileged world than me. My
privilege was to have known life without privilege.

BETWEEN TWO WORLDS

I'D LEAVE ON SATURDAY AFTERNOON WITHOUT KNOW-
ing where I would sleep that night, and get back to Amiens on
Sunday evening or Monday morning. In bars I almost always
met someone who'd invite me to spend the night at his place;
I'd understood right from the first weekend that it was simple
enough to meet someone and find a place to sleep. The fear
that otherwise I'd have to spend the night outside made the
need to meet someone stronger, more violent, and so more
beautiful. But sometimes I failed, sometimes I didn't meet
anyone; on those evenings I walked all night after the bars had
closed, in the cold, my body exhausted and with dark circles
under my eyes, I wandered through the streets I didn't know,
in this city I hadn't yet got to know, until six in the morning,
before taking the first train back to Amiens, my body trembling with cold and fatigue—but I wasn't sad, above all I felt
the pleasure of the new life that would begin with my move
and that was already starting, the sensation of having adven-
tures and doing things that just six months earlier I would
never have thought possible.

(I should also talk about sexuality, and the thrill in Paris of suddenly being able to meet an almost unlimited number of men and to finally live, even more radically and easily than in Amiens, to have what I had desired since my birth, the feeling of bodily freedom and of entering, thanks to sexuality, myriad new universes.)

When I went out in Paris it was almost always to the same bar, the Duplex, in a narrow street, a little way away from the other bars, because Didier, whom I'd meet in the afternoon in the cafés of Montparnasse on those weekends, had told me that it was an *intellectual bar*. It was poorly lit, there was a smell of sweat and beer inside that gave it a cinematic thickness and depth. I'd spot a man in the shadows of the bar. I realize now that I always singled out the men who looked the most distinguished, the ones who seemed the richest; my social desire blended with my sexual desire, I was attracted to men who looked like they were part of the world I'd wanted to belong to ever since I'd decided to leave Amiens, the ones who were the most in keeping with my dream of transformation. There was no need for me to consciously think that these men belonged to this world for me to approach them, to desire them, since I was *physically* attracted to them. There was no difference between my physical and my social desire.

When a man I was talking to asked me what my parents did for a living—it's a strange thing to ask someone you've just met in a bar, but they asked it, often even, as if to size me up and make sure they weren't wasting their time—I answered that my father was a lawyer or a professor. I was ashamed, I thought that if I told the truth they'd lose interest. If they wanted more details, I'd talk about Elena's parents as if they were my own. I'd steal Elena's life, steal her parents and say that my father taught at the university and my mother had been an actress—but most of the time I'd say I didn't want to talk about my family.

Back in Amiens after my trips to Paris I didn't tell Elena anything about what I'd done there. She'd say: *One day one of the men you meet there will separate us forever.* I pretended not to hear.

ÉCOLE NORMALE SUPÉRIEURE

I WAS EMBARKING ON A NEW PROCESS OF TRANSFORMA-
tion. Starting all over again like that without knowing if I was
going to succeed, I needed a definitive act, something that
would mark a clean break with Amiens and compensate for
the uncertainty of what I was seeking to become. This break
was writing a book, I was sure of it now, but I also knew that
to write one I'd need time.

I worked out plans and strategies to accelerate my change,
and it was while I was reflecting on them that I first dared
to think about the École Normale Supérieure as a possibility.
It had already struck me that a large number of the authors
I was reading, and whose works Didier had recommended
to me, Jacques Derrida, Pierre Bourdieu, Michel Foucault,
Jean-Paul Sartre, had been students at this same school
in Paris. I learned that it was one of the most prestigious
schools in France—I'd never even heard of it. Suddenly
it dawned on me that if I arrived in Paris without going
to this school I'd be nothing but a young man from

Amiens, a marooned intruder, whereas going there would legitimize my presence in the city, as if Paris was the name of a reality greater than that encompassed by the city's perimeter.

After a few days of looking into the matter I spoke to Elena about it. She said that of course she knew about the École Normale Supérieure. During her whole childhood her mother had hoped, without totally believing it, that Elena would become a student there. *You need a very high level of education to get in, it's made for kids of the Parisian upper classes who've attended the best lycées, not for us.*

For the first time, Elena's "us" was on the side of the dominated, not the dominant.

I listened to her and promised myself that one day I'd do it, I'd enter that school.

Paradoxically, her resignation gave me strength. I refused to accept—naively, but later I'd understand that naivety is a condition of escape—that something could be impossible. I kept inquiring and discovered that you could enter the École Normale by several routes; reviewing all of the conditions for admission, I contemplated the inaccessible.

When I saw Didier again I told him of my plan. I had to gather my strength to overcome the fear of ridicule and tell him that I wanted to try to get admitted to this school—in fact by the least prestigious route, the only one possible for someone like me, who only a few weeks earlier had never heard of it and hadn't gone to one of the lycées that Elena had talked about but wasn't thinking about at the time.

Didier smiled, *You're ambitious, that's good. Sure, go ahead. Give it a try.*

PREPARATION

ÉCOLE NORMALE SUPÉRIEURE. FOR SEVERAL MONTHS I thought about nothing but this goal, in fear and dread. I thought, *If you get into that school you'll never go back to the village.* It wasn't the studies themselves or the things I'd learn there that interested me, but the knowledge that if I entered this school there could be no turning back.

Through Didier I'd become aware that my diploma from the University of Amiens alone would not help me get in. He knew this because at my age he too had fallen victim to the same illusion: children from the poorest backgrounds see entering university as a consecration, but in fact university degrees, especially if they're obtained in small towns, have long since lost any value they had.

In his book *Returning to Reims* he wrote: "A simple lack of knowledge regarding the hierarchical structure of educational institutions and a lack of understanding of how processes of selection operate might lead people to make counterproductive choices, to choose paths that lead nowhere, nonetheless imagining that they are lucky to have gotten to a place in which people who know what they are doing would be sure never to end up. This is how people from less advantaged classes end up believing that they are gaining access to what has previously been denied to them, whereas in reality, once they have that access, it turns out to mean very little, because the system has evolved and the important and valuable place to be has now shifted somewhere else. The processes of being pushed out or excluded may here be operating more slowly, or happening at a later date, but the division between those in dominant positions and those in dominated ones remains intact. It reproduces itself by changing location."

Entering the École Normale meant saving myself from this mistake.

I got cracking. I had to prepare a research project and then take an oral exam to have a chance of achieving what had now become a real-life fantasy for me, the promise of a better life. A large number of candidates were eliminated at the first stage on the basis of their research project, so I worked on it for several months; I didn't tell anyone in Amiens, not even Elena, I was afraid she'd think that I was aiming too high, that my ambitions were disproportionate and therefore ridiculous; I didn't tell anyone else either, because I was afraid of their laughter, which would have nailed me to the past. I needed letters of recommendation and Didier offered to write one for me, I kept attending all of his lectures at the University of Amiens.

Above all I prepared by continuing to read as many books as possible. I read at night, during meals, frenetically absorbing all the books Didier had recommended to me as well as others I'd discovered myself, each reading experience engendering another, each book leading me to another—and each book taking me further from my past self. I saw Didier from the time he left his lectures to the time he boarded the evening train back to Paris. As I watched it pull away I tried to imagine the life of secrets and mysteries hidden behind the word Paris, the life that my short trips there had not been enough to unveil. I thought: *Soon that word will be my life. Soon I too will be a mystery to others, to those who have remained here.*

When we met for a coffee Didier would give me reading suggestions, or he'd email them to me in the evening.

Didier ERIBON   August 12, 2010   ↰ ...
to me ⌄

you can also read Frantz Fanon: BLACK SKIN, WHITE MASKS . . .

And if you have time: books by Jean Genet: THE THIEF'S JOURNAL, OUR LADY OF THE FLOWERS.

And of course (but this will take time): Sartre's SAINT GENET.

You can also read Marcel Jouhandeau: DE L'ABJECTION (it's quite magnificent, leaving aside the Christian moralism, which is a bit invasive, but which sets the framework for his reflection on the very

beautiful idea of self-invention through the insults one
receives).

For a theoretical reflection: Bourdieu: PASCALIAN
MEDITATIONS.

There . . . that should get you through to the start of
the school year!!!

...

When Didier spoke I didn't just listen to him, I absorbed
his every word, his every gesture. (One day, several years after
these moments with him—that is, when all the energy, struggle and despair had become memory—I'll remember that the
first time I met him in a café in the center of town he asked
the waiter in a muted, gentle voice for an espresso and a glass
of water, and for months afterward I ordered the same thing
whenever I could, whenever the chance arose: ordering coffee
and water, in the same hushed voice Didier had used, seemed
to me a sign of extreme distinction, a sign that one belonged to
a class that was inaccessible to me—and to which I wanted to
belong, precisely because of its inaccessibility.)

But for now I had to focus on the entrance requirements
for the École Normale, and write the research project. I had
no idea where to start, so I proceeded as I'd always done
when I wanted to change: I imitated. I'd read somewhere that
Jean-Paul Sartre read a book a day when he was young, and
I thought I should do the same. I read much of the night to
maintain this humanly impossible rhythm, Elena thought I
looked tired and said I was losing weight. Based on these read-

ings I sketched out how I'd approach writing the project, I explained my ideas to Didier and he gave me advice, naming other books I could read, *Keep going, keep going.* And I kept going, visiting the school's website every day and even several times a day, gazing at the photos of the buildings, the court-yard, the fountain towering in the middle of the courtyard, and praying let me be accepted, a prayer as simple and banal as that, without knowing exactly to whom this *let me* was addressed.

I asked Babeth for extra hours at the Maison de la Culture so I could earn more money to buy more books, I worked, I bought books, I read them, the lack of sleep accumulated in my muscles but I told myself that I'd rest later, once I was saved for good; rest had become a promise.

LUDOVIC

I KEPT GOING TO PARIS ON WEEKENDS. I'D MANAGED TO find a way of pairing the vital need to meet men with the physical need to work; I arrived on Saturday by train and walked from the Gare du Nord to a municipal library that stayed open until late; there I worked, that is I read, I read until my eyes hurt, I took notes and tried to memorize them for the oral exam—if it came to that. I bought notebooks and filled them. I was driven by the energy of despair, I had the feeling that if I didn't read all the books in the world, if I didn't know everything there was to know, I'd fail, I had to catch up with all those who would be part of my new life in Paris and whom I saw all around me during my sessions in the library, those who unlike me had been reading since the first years of their lives, who had intellectual and cultural references that were foreign to me, references I didn't so much as suspect, I no longer saw my life as anything but a race I'd joined too late, when everyone else had almost crossed the finish line, I had to make up for this impossible delay. *I must save myself.* Around eight in the evening I'd go down to the courtyard and eat a sandwich I'd made in Amiens before taking the train, then I'd go back up to my desk between the stacks, and when the library closed later on—it was almost always late at night when I left—I'd head for the bar district where I knew I could find what I was looking for, someone to spend the night with, someone at whose place I could sleep. I'd walk dazed from hours of reading and concentration, the new concepts and ideas throbbing in my temples.

I'd sleep with a stranger, almost always someone new, and at noon on Sunday I'd go back to the library and work all day long as I'd done the day before. On Sunday evening I'd return to Amiens, my head full not only of all I'd learned but also of all the people I'd met, the flats I'd entered, the men who'd invited me back to their place, a football player who'd taken me to his home in the distant suburbs and told me to say I was a friend from work if we met anyone he knew, a banker who lived in an immense apartment, a failed photographer. When I went back to Amiens on Sunday as the sun was setting it was like returning to the past, to everything that I wanted to be a part of the past, as if my feelings were getting ahead of reality and Amiens was already my past although it was still my present, and Paris was my present although it was still only my future—a future that was for now merely virtual, potential.

It was in one of the bars in the Marais district where I often went looking for someone at whose place I could sleep that I met Ludovic. I grew close to him quickly, because I was touched by how kind he was to me and because he corresponded to what I wanted to become; he taught at a big Parisian university, he traveled, he had money, he was fully

integrated into Paris life. He went to the theater, the opera. I
wanted him to take me into his life, like Elena and Didier had
done. He invited me to sleep at his place, to spend evenings
with him in luxurious restaurants with soft lighting and where
often the chef would come out to greet us at the end of the
meal. Ludovic told me that was a sign of distinction, with him
I continued the transformation of myself. Other times he'd
take me to a hotel. He said that sleeping in a hotel gave him
a sense of freedom, and it was strange to think of people in
my childhood who didn't eat every day for want of money,
while other people slept in a hotel just to get a *sense of freedom*.
Thanks to Ludovic, I didn't have to look for a place to spend
the night when I arrived in Paris on Saturday afternoon. I'd
work in the library during the day, and in the evening I'd join
him. On Sundays he'd take me to lunch in tea rooms where
you could drink tea and champagne during the same meal.
These meals were called brunches, I didn't know the word.
(Today I have to ask myself: was I using Ludovic? Did I get
close to him because I understood that he could help me in
my projected arrival in Paris? I don't think so.)

I talked to Ludovic about the École Normale Supérieure;
he'd studied there, and he gave me advice on how to write my
project and deal with the oral exam I'd have to take if I passed
the first stage. Sometimes on Saturday afternoons I saw Didier
but I was still too intimidated by him and after each meeting I felt burdened by melancholy. Everything he'd achieved,
the books he'd written, his status as a famous intellectual, all
weighed on me because it reminded me of everything I was
not. He'd introduced me to his younger partner Geoffroy,
who was also starting to write books.

PROJECT, WRAP-UP (HOPE)

ONE DAY THE PROJECT WAS FINISHED. I'D WORKED ON IT for over a year, a year dreaming of leaving for Paris. I reread what I'd written several times, printed it out at Geoffroy's place, collected all the necessary admission documents and walked to the buildings of the École Normale. It was a Friday afternoon, I'd come to Paris a day earlier than usual. I'd dressed as well as I could, in my best shirt and tie, squeezed into a waistcoat and jacket; I took the metro and when I got to the school courtyard I was still thinking: *if you make it in here you're saved.* I didn't notice that I was the only one dressed like that, so formally, I'd tried to dress the way I thought students at this kind of school dressed. I knocked on a door and a small brunette woman asked me to come in; I smiled; I wanted her to like me. She took my file and I asked her how many applications like that she'd received. "A few hundred," she said, "and in your section only two or three will be admitted so the competition is tough!" I don't remember what I replied, I imagine something banal like "I'll keep my fingers crossed." I went out and thought, I'll make it.

I had to wait for the results but I knew that even if I didn't get in I'd still move to Paris in the autumn.

I went to Paris more and more often, my presence in Amiens was limited to the two or three days a week I spent with Elena, but every day I resembled her a little less, we were growing further and further apart. When we got together during the week I had the impression I was seeing the person I'd been before, as if she were a photograph of my past.

I struggled to get her to embrace my transformation and transform herself along with me. I told her about the books I was reading and encouraged her to read them as well; I urged her to adopt my new lifestyle, I invited her to come and have brunch with me, to dress in a way I imagined was more Parisian. It was as if the images of my beginnings in Amiens were reversed, now I was the one trying to transform her, but I was failing. Did she subconsciously resent me for this reversal and the fact that now I was the one teaching things to her? I told her about my plans, about Paris, and asked her to come and live with me; but the more I changed, the more she saw me change and the more she hardened and clung to what she was—that is, what I had been. We argued, she shouted that she despised Parisians and their snobbery, and that if I continued to become like them she'd end up despising me too. She hated my blind, naive adherence to the rules of the bourgeoisie. During our arguments she shouted that she wanted to read for pleasure and not to accumulate knowledge and power the way I did; she'd given me my first books, she'd taken me to see my first arthouse films, and now she was saying that all these things disgusted her, that she didn't want to be like me.

Still I insisted; I wanted her to meet Didier, I thought that if she got to know him she might change her mind and want to come and live in Paris with me.

I brought them together in a café; I'd told Didier that Elena was my best friend, and we talked for an hour. Didier asked her questions. He was trying to get to know her but she didn't answer in her usual way; I could see she was suffering. When we'd finished our drinks, I said to Didier that I could take the bus to the station with him—he was going back to Paris that evening. Elena walked with us to the bus stop, I said goodbye to her and when the bus drove off with Didier and me inside, Elena gave him the finger, her face twisted in an expression of pain and sadness.

RESULT

THE NEWS ARRIVED ONE MORNING IN AMIENS, WHEN I woke up. I opened my eyes, went to the kitchen and discovered that I'd received a letter announcing that I'd been selected for the oral exam. I wept, and called Didier to tell him. I spoke quickly, uncontrollably. I went for a walk in the city and looked around me, I stared at the brick houses and the streets as if I was seeing them for the last time, I was saying goodbye, I wanted to remember everything, photograph everything.

The test was scheduled for just one week later and for a week I read as much as I could, I prepared sentences, wrote down ideas on different subjects, and practiced speaking in front of the mirror. I asked Léa and Lucas to replace me at the Maison de la Culture, I had to spend all my time preparing for the oral exam, and of course they accepted, even though I hadn't explained to them why I couldn't come to work; I told them that it was important without saying more. (I haven't mentioned it yet, but I didn't tell the people around me in

Amiens about the test because I was afraid to fail and if I did I'd have to tell them, and—stupidly—I'd have felt that in admitting my failure I was admitting my weakness.)

I went to Paris the day before the test. Didier had advised me to come a day earlier to prepare with him and Geoffroy, I followed his advice, they played the jury and asked me questions, the two of them sitting on Geoffroy's bed and me standing in front of them. I tried to answer as well as I could, but after each of my answers I thought: *I'll never do it.* That evening I slept in a hotel. Didier had reserved a room for me so I could spend the night comfortably before the test the next day, he'd paid for it, and as with Babeth, Ludovic and in a way Elena I wonder: why did he decide to take responsibility for my destiny? Did I evoke this response in people, were the infinite despair and limitless hope that coexisted in me visible?

In the metro on the way to the École Normale a single sentence hammered through my body, always the same: *If you make it in you're saved.* I tried to think of something else but I couldn't escape myself, the words and the reality behind them were stronger than I was, nothing could displace the thought, *If you make it in you're saved.*

I was wearing a shirt and jacket but Didier had said I shouldn't wear a tie, too formal. I got off the metro and walked up the stairs to the street, and then the couple of hundred meters to the school. When I arrived at the entrance my legs became heavy, walking was too difficult, as if suddenly I was walking in an ocean against the current or wading through a river of clay. The corners of my lips trembled, I tried to smile at the people around me but my smile changed to a quiver. All the students I passed in the corridors seemed better-looking than me, more intelligent than me, I could see it written on their bodies that they belonged to a privileged world, I'd learned to see such things at a glance, I could see their whole childhood in details as minute and circumstantial as their posture or the way they combed their hair, I could see the journeys they'd taken as children, their conversations with their parents, the books they'd read at six or seven, the food they'd eaten simply in the way they looked at others, their whole history was written on them, you just had to know how to read it and I did, I'd acquired that power. A man called out my name in the corridor, Mr. Bellegueule? Several people turned toward me, they must have thought it was a joke, they must have thought that nobody could have such a ridiculous name. My legs felt even heavier, I was afraid I'd collapse on the floor and be unable to move, that I'd ruin everything at this point, after months of work and effort, when I was closer to the goal than ever.

In front of the panel I started to believe I could do it after all.

I remembered everything I'd learned, all the notes I'd written on cards in the previous months, the advice given to me by Didier and Geoffroy, our mock test the day before; everything came back. I spoke effortlessly, with ease and confidence I believe, the fear was gone. The man who'd asked me the most questions thanked me and I left. I was sure I'd passed, I called Didier to tell him what had happened but he curbed my enthusiasm, today I understand that he did it out of generosity, he wanted to cushion my fall in case I'd failed.

A few days later I received a letter telling me that I'd been admitted. I fell to my knees, I wept again, everything was changing around me, the meaning of my past and future, my view of my life and of others, even the quality of the air and the light seemed to be transformed. I kept repeating to myself: *I'm saved, I'm saved.*

IMAGINARY CONVERSATION IN FRONT OF A MIRROR

**From that moment on you must have been more impatient to
leave Amiens than ever.**

It was more than impatience. The closer my departure for
Paris drew, the more I suffocated in Amiens; I felt trapped.
The certainty of the future—and by that I mean the certainty that I'd go to Paris to study in this school that was
for me, as I've told you, the sign of a definitive rupture—
made the reality of the present unbearable. Being accepted
there accentuated my feeling of escaping, as if I'd be more
in Paris at the École Normale than if I studied elsewhere,
as if Paris wasn't the name of a city but of a certain social reality, and in going to this school I'd be even more
there—do you see what I mean?

I didn't know yet that once I'd entered this school it
would no longer have any importance for me.

I invited Elena to have a drink with me on the terrace

of a café, the weather was nice, it was a hot, late-summer day. I sat down opposite her and announced that I was moving, that I'd be leaving for Paris in a month. She knew that my plans to leave Amiens were panning out, but she hadn't imagined that everything would happen so quickly, I think. And then I told her that I'd prepared for the entrance exam at the École Normale Supérieure for months without telling her, and that I'd been accepted.

How did she react?

I don't remember. All I remember is how torn I felt. I still loved her, but I felt that the I who thought "I still love her" was not the I who had loved her. I'd changed too much, I was no longer the same person. And yet I loved her. It's difficult to explain . . . I was trying to hold on tight to our relationship, but I realized that a relationship never really exists as such, I was learning this obvious fact, it's a bond between two people and I was no longer that person, the one who'd been in the relationship with Elena. I was clutching at shadows.

I'd have liked to implore Elena to change too, and follow my lead, to adopt my new dreams, my new centers of interest. I wanted to shake her by the shoulders and order her to become like me, to shout in her face that she should want to live in Paris, to live every possible life, to change from top to bottom like me . . .

She broke the news to Nadya and Nadya prepared a small party in my honor; Elena's sister made a cake for the occasion, with the letters ENS written on the chocolate icing.

It should have been a celebration, but the whole evening tasted like ashes.

Inevitably the evening turned into a dirge, a separation ceremony.

And then?

Word got out. I'd told several people that I was leaving, and why. And then I saw on the Internet that people—people I'd known for several years and with whom I'd been friends— were saying that I'd slept with Didier to "succeed"—it's a ridiculous word, but it's the one they used. They said I was ambitious, egotistical, a social climber, that I'd taken advantage of my friends in Amiens and everything I'd learned there just so I could leave and go to Paris. When I walked down the street I felt people's hostile glances—I know what I'm saying will sound far-fetched but it's true. The rumors multiplied, each one engendering another that was even bigger and uglier. Why did these people react like that? In wanting to change had I reminded them of exactly what they were not doing? Is it arrogant of me even to ask the question? No it's not, because I don't believe that those who change are superior to those who don't, at the time I did, okay, but not anymore . . . I try to understand. Maybe a hatred for change, without cause or explanation, is trans- mitted between bodies and through time. I don't know.

How did you react to these rumors?

I couldn't find the words. I was paralyzed. I could only scream when I was alone.

I remember there was this one girl, Clothilde, who'd

gone to the lycée with Elena and me, who from that day on wrote on the social networks that I'd taken advantage of everything Elena and her family had given me, their culture, their knowledge of art and the cinema. What could I say to that? The accusation was so ugly that it reduced me to silence. I could only think: I have to leave, I have to leave.

FAREWELLS

I'D ALREADY STARTED LOOKING FOR A PLACE TO LIVE IN
Paris. I didn't have enough money to rent a flat and I'd filled
out the forms to apply for a room in a university residence. I
was telling Ludovic about these formalities when he offered to
let me live at his place. Night was falling, Ludovic was walking on my left, pushing his bike, which he almost always had
with him. In addition to the large flat where he lived with his
children he owned a small studio in the center of Paris near
the Place de la République. I could stay in the studio for free,
I wouldn't have to pay any rent. His offer changed everything,
the future seemed almost doable, everything was falling into
place. I took Ludovic in my arms and kissed him on the cheek.

Moving day was approaching. In Amiens I counted the
days before I left, I thought: *only twenty-one days left, you can
do it, only twenty days and you'll be out of here.* I'd filled about
ten cardboard boxes, I had nothing but my clothes and the
books I'd bought since I met Didier. I'd resigned from the
Maison de la Culture, Babeth had given me a big hug; she told

me that she was proud of me, that she was sure I'd do great
things in Paris, she was one of the few people in Amiens who
was happy for me, she and my co-workers Christiane, Satine,
Lucas, Léa and the rest, I don't know why the people there
were so different from the world around them, maybe because
most of them were artists and they saw this work at the theater
as a stage in their lives, because they too hoped to leave one
day and this hope was contained in their presence. Elena
needed money and I'd asked Babeth to hire her in my place,
Babeth trusted me and promised she would (and she kept her
promise the week after I left).

It was time to say goodbye to Elena. I met her on the terrace of a café. She was waiting for me, I could see her from
a distance, her phone and a glass on the table in front of her.
The sun was too strong, it attacked my skin and dried my
mouth. I sat down and looked at Elena, but couldn't think of
anything to say. The sun was burning me. I tried anyway, and
asked her once again to come with me, *We'll have Ludovic's
flat, we'll be together. You'll be able to do whatever you want.*

She told me again that her life wasn't in Paris, but here. I
didn't insist. I stayed there beside her without saying a thing.
People were walking and laughing on the pavement, the sun
on their skin made them smile. I searched for something to
say, just one sentence, but the more I searched, the more the
possibility of finding one seemed to recede. I tried not to cry
because I knew that tears would make my departure more
real, my leaving her more real. Images flooded back to me
in the silence: the first time I saw her, when Romain pointed

her out at school; the first time I sat next to her in the library, fascinated by her ability to concentrate; of our dunk in the icy sea, the first time I danced with her and smelled her hair, times when her sonorous laughter filled whatever room she was in. I remembered the night when I'd drunk too much and slept snuggled against her in her tiny bed, warmed by her skin, barely conscious but reassured by her presence; the time I'd nearly died of peritonitis and she'd spent two weeks at my bedside, feeding me, wiping my sweat-covered forehead. I thought: *don't cry, do not cry.* I didn't know what Elena was thinking as she sat there next to me, I imagine she was mad at me. After almost an hour with no one saying a word, I got up and said I had to go. It was over.

In an early version of this book I started with the words:

The story of my life is a succession of broken friendships. At each stage of this life, of this race against myself, I've had to break with people I loved in order to move forward. I didn't decide to, neither did they: I was struggling to transform myself, they didn't have the same obsession, they remained the way they were when I met them, and suddenly we no longer resembled one another; we had nothing to say to one another, we no longer understood one another. All that remained for me to do was look for new people who would welcome me into their lives, before my desire to change pushed me toward yet another life, and to abandon them in turn.

A MONOLOGUE BY ELENA
(tribute to Jean-Luc Lagarce)

When you left
—I remember everything—
I had to get my head around it. I had to understand that
    I wasn't your life, but that I'd only been a moment in
    your life.
And that I'd been wrong.

Am I to blame?
Maybe I did something bad,
I don't know
You could have told me.
Why didn't you tell me
you could have told me
if I did or said something bad,
A mistake

I would have changed.
I could have changed.
You can't just walk away without giving the other person
     a chance to improve.
It's not fair.
Do you hear me?
Why didn't you give me a chance?

No I didn't make a mistake
I don't know why I'm saying these
     things
I let myself be taken in,
as they say,
I talk but I know
I know the answer
And the answer is You.

It wasn't my mistakes that made you leave but your
     egotism,
The answer isn't in me
It's entirely outside of me
I mustn't be confused about that
I mustn't let myself be manipulated
You wanted to live your life,
You yourself said it when I chided you
It was your way of not answering
I have to live my life
And for you I was just a stage on the way.

I should have noticed.

I wanted to be your destination and I was only the
     starting point.

It's silly,
I thought I'd spend my life with you.
We talked about it, we dreamed,
You'd be a history teacher and I'd be a journalist or an artist,
Not a great artist,
no,
that didn't interest me,
I've never dreamed of fame,
Just a small artist in a small provincial town,
With something to do,
An artist without an audience,
But we'd have been happy.

I'd have been happy.

Why did you leave?

I'm left with images
You walking in the rain beside me
You singing in my ear
You whispering
You being here

Do you remember the time you showed up with your
     face covered in makeup?
It was in front of the cathedral
You thought you were ugly, I always had to reassure you
     about that

And that day,
You'd decided to put on makeup because you hated your
    face.

When I saw you coming with your orange face
—you didn't know how to put on makeup, you'd never
    done it before—
I laughed.
I couldn't stop laughing
You were ridiculously orange,
I looked at you and laughed,
But my laughter didn't hurt you,
You remember
You weren't hurt
You who were always so touchy
and got offended for nothing
You laughed with me.
I said: Look at you, you're orange!

I took a tissue from my pocket, wet it with my spit and
    cleaned your face.
I held your face in one hand and the tissue in the other
You let me do it
And I said to you: don't hide. You're handsome, you don't
    need to hide.
Don't hide

It's too late now
All these images will disappear.

IS IT PRETENTIOUS OF ME TO IMAGINE ELENA'S PAIN? IN fact it's my own pain, regrets and nostalgia that I'm putting into words I imagine coming from her. It's the Other Me, the one who would have liked to stay, who's speaking, and who in speaking takes me to task.

ARRIVAL

JULIETTE, THE NEW FRIEND ELENA AND I HAD MET AT the university, had packed my boxes into her car; I took the train and she met me in Paris. I waited for her downstairs at Ludovic's flat, she arrived and we lugged up the boxes—in the space of an afternoon the move was complete. Ludovic had left a tiny table, a chair and a sofa bed in the flat, I put my books on the floor and arranged my clothes in the little cupboard. Juliette spent the night together with her fiancé, Guillaume, the three of us squeezed into the sofa bed, the next day they drove back to Amiens, and when I found myself alone in the studio I looked around and thought: This is your home now. You live in Paris. Everything can start.

I wandered through the streets and observed the people around me. I told myself that I lived in this city, I was now one of the people I'd envied when I'd seen them walking around Paris with their shopping bags a few months earlier, people whose lives I could only guess at, and now seen from the outside one could perhaps have thought that I too had always been part of this life, that I'd always been here in this city, and envied me in turn. When I came back up to the flat I took a sheet of paper and wrote down the program for my life to come:

Change my name (go to court?), Change my face, Change my skin (tattoo?),
Read (become someone else, write), Change my body, Change my habits, Change my life (become someone).

I don't know if it's the same for everyone, but for me when the process of my transformation began it was more than just a conscious effort, it became a permanent obsession.

Some people describe their transformation as a slow undertaking, a superposition of successive changes in their body and its states, in their way of being and existing that was so staggered and diffused in time that it didn't take a conscious effort on their part for them to achieve themselves; others explain that it was through contact with other types of bodies and individuals than those they'd known in the first part of their lives that they changed, by internalizing—often in a diffuse way—the attitudes of these new bodies and individuals. That wasn't my case. I wanted to change everything, and I wanted everything about my change to be the result of a decision. I wanted nothing to escape my willpower.

Looking to the left out of the window in Ludovic's little flat I observed the sky, the roofs of the buildings and the bodies far off in the street, and I thought, "Everything is starting."

III

SHORT LETTERS FOR A LONG FAREWELL

(fictional conversations with Elena)

IN THE FIRST DAYS WHEN I ARRIVED IN PARIS I FELT THE freedom of beginnings, one so special that it can't be compared with any other form of freedom, like what I experienced with you when I moved into the flat on Boulevard Carnot. I'd wake up in the morning and look at the sofa bed where I was lying, the kitchen, the little table and matching chair where I could work and eat, the books I'd brought from Amiens and think: I'm home. I'm free.

I thought: I could never have hoped to get this far.

I was afraid to tell you about it at the time because I didn't want to put more distance between us than necessary, but it was as if everything was beautiful in Paris, I can tell you that today, the years have passed, everything was beautiful, even the most insignificant things: buying water at the corner shop, taking my clothes to the launderette, buying cleaning products, even the worst, most banal and boring things like filling out administrative forms, because everything I did was like a confirmation of my freedom and the proof that I'd succeeded.

[Did you miss me?]

I continued to explore Paris as I'd done during my first trips, when the capital was still no more than a dream, I went to bed when I wanted, I read, I met men, I went to classes at the École Normale with the heady, naive feeling of belonging to an elite, all these everyday gestures I experienced as if I was defying fate.

I was trying to forget you. *I had to live every possible life*, I kept repeating to myself, and I think I told myself it was this imperative, not me or my decisions but something stronger than me, something of which I was not the cause, that had driven us apart. By the nature of things I should have known nothing but life in northern France, I told myself, since no one I'd grown up with had been able to escape it, you know that, they grew up and died in the region where they were born, and every day I felt buoyed by the elation of a survivor. I remembered how guys from the village would announce that they were going to live somewhere else, in a big city, to become cooks or waiters, the only jobs available to them without diplomas or knowledge, only to return a few weeks later, grumbling with downcast eyes that they'd failed, that it was too difficult, too expensive, that they'd lost their jobs, as if the village had reclaimed them. I, by contrast, wanted to miss out on nothing. Living everything meant taking revenge for the place the world had assigned me at birth. And that—am I wrong?—you didn't understand.

All you could see was that you'd been abandoned.

I'd met a fashion designer in a bar. It was just after the move. He invited me to sleep at his place during the week and had me pose for photo shoots, he said I should become a model. He introduced me to his friends who all worked in the same milieu, they traveled from continent to continent and switched from French to English when they spoke, it's funny, *they were always coming back from somewhere,* from Italy, Singapore, South Korea. Around eight in the evening they'd get together and party. They'd put on dance music and take turns going into the bathroom to snort cocaine, they'd offer me some, I'd dance with them, the music would pulse through my body, I'd drink champagne and vodka until morning. And there were evenings—this is what I'm getting at—when I stopped, looked around me as if I could freeze time and thought that I'd never expected to live so much, in the most quantitative sense of the word, so many experiences, so many sensations, so many scenes that were so far removed from the ones I'd shared with you or with my family when I was younger. And there were other encounters, other lives, a railway worker who joined me at night with the smell of grease and metal on his body, a man who invited me to dine in the greatest palace hotels, the Ritz, the Plaza Athénée— you should have seen my body, my way of speaking in those places!—another who sold drugs and always carried around wads of cash, another who took me to the biggest opera festivals in Europe, Salzburg and Aix-en-Provence.

I was living everything.

Above all I kept seeing Ludovic. He was the one who'd made my arrival in Paris so easy, and had given me a place to live. When I told you that at the beginning, before silence fell between us for good, you said I was manipulating him to gain access to the world of Paris, but it's not true, I wasn't manipulating him, I wanted him to help me, it's different. Maybe I said things to him that I didn't completely mean, maybe I flattered him a bit, but it wasn't to hurt him, it wasn't cynicism that made me act like that but the need—almost the desperation—to be helped. People who're just trying to get by are always seen as manipulators, but nothing could be further from the truth, Elena. You said I liked him because he helped me but such distinctions make no sense, of course I liked him partly for that, not just for that but also for that, because that's how he appeared to me, that's what he was, someone who could help me, just like you can be someone who's beautiful, or sensitive, or intelligent. Is it forbidden to appreciate someone for the protection he gives you?

He told me he liked being with me. I think he understood what was happening, my sudden desire to know the world, and he wanted to be part of this rebirth. On weekends he'd take me on trips to Lisbon, Rome, London, Porto, Istanbul. I'd never been anywhere before and now I was traveling everywhere with him, through him I discovered unknown aspects of human existence. I visited museums, cathedrals, mosques; he gave me novels written by authors from the countries we visited, Pessoa in Portugal, D'Annunzio in Italy, Woolf in England. I'd become bourgeois, I was living the life and I almost looked the part. No one could see my past beneath the surface of my disguise, at least that's what I wanted to believe. The wonderment I felt on my first visits to Paris was multiplied tenfold, I'd take a plane and think I was never meant to take one, I was never destined to fly, I'd sit in a restaurant in Lisbon opposite Ludovic and think I was never meant to be here, I'd look at the Acropolis in Athens and think My eyes were never meant to see this, I was overwhelmed by the miracle of every step I took, I was an intruder who'd stolen a life that wasn't his. In writing this I'm writing my own *Thief's Journal*. One morning in Rome, in a room that Ludovic had rented for us in the Villa Medici, I was reading Louis-Ferdinand Céline's *Journey to the End of the Night*, the book you were reading when I first met you, and seeing myself there in that room in Italy, reading the book that was a symbol of my escape, suddenly made me cry. Ludovic had gone out to get coffee. I wiped my eyes for fear of being ridiculous, and when he came back I didn't tell him what had happened.

[I missed you.]

I STARTED WORKING RIGHT AFTER I MOVED IN. I HAD TO
write, that was why I'd moved away from Amiens and from
you, and in a way I had no choice, I had to make sense of my
escape.

I knew how I should go about it from my Tuesday dinners
with Didier in Amiens before I left. He'd described his sched-
ule, how he organized it, how much time he spent writing each
day. I worked for the same number of hours, I did the same
things, writing, printing, making corrections on paper, rewrit-
ing, reprinting, starting over with new corrections. I played at
writing the way I'd played at being you. Basically, in writing
I was performing gestures that took me away from the past, I
wrote in the same way I'd learned to laugh in front of a mirror, I wrote to fend off fate. I'd sit in front of the computer
and concentrate. I'd spoken to Didier and Geoffroy about my
childhood and they'd urged me to write about what I'd experienced, the exclusion at school, my family, the village; so
I tried. When I woke up I'd drink a few cups of coffee, often

with Ludovic, then I'd turn on the computer and string words together but I couldn't make them gel, everything I wrote was weak, it all sounded wrong, my sentences were both heavy and hollow (didactic-elliptic, Didier said with a laugh). I tried for a month, two months, every day at the same rhythm, but I was unable to produce a single usable sentence, and gave up.

I didn't tell you that I'd quit. I didn't tell you that in fact at that moment the euphoria of the first weeks in Paris had dissipated completely, and not just because of my failure at writing. I didn't tell you because I was afraid of proving you right, of hearing you tell me that I shouldn't have left. When I spoke to you I'd say that everything was fine and that I was living a magnificent, enviable life, that I was writing a book, but that was just to conceal what was really happening. Because I saw that in Paris I'd have to start my metamorphosis all over again. Because everything I'd learned in Amiens was no longer of any use, in Paris I was in a new world and everywhere I went I did not fit in. In Amiens, with you, I'd felt like I belonged to the city's small elite, like I'd got somewhere in the world, in Paris I was no longer anything at all, nothing I'd learned was worth a thing.

What you also don't know is that even at the École Normale Supérieure I didn't get along with the others. I felt as far from them as I'd felt from people in Amiens when I arrived from the village. I couldn't relate to what they talked about, I felt stupid, awkward, uncouth. Most of them had been born into families of lawyers, architects, businessmen or professors, they'd grown up in the most beautiful parts of Paris, and in their company I felt myself reverting to the very first years of my life, with nothing to go on, no knowledge and no past on which I could draw, I felt I was backpedaling in relation to Amiens, the students in Paris sent me reeling into the past— I can't say you didn't warn me. They quoted authors I didn't know, they talked about trips they'd taken with their families, they looked so very at ease with their bodies, when I compared myself with them I felt ashamed of my broken, random trajectory. It's silly, I remember when a light cut out in a corridor, all of a sudden it was dark and a student exclaimed: How outré! It was a mystery to me how in his surprise he could have uttered such a sophisticated and formal word, I could never have done the same, despite my transformation with you. My presence at the school became a source of distress and melancholy, and I decided to go there as little as possible. I went to my classes, but I contrived to leave as soon as they were over.

Around that time you wrote to me in anger, describing how you imagined me strutting down the corridors between sociology seminars and philosophy classes, swollen with pride in my new life.

I want you to know that you were wrong.

I want you to know that my life wasn't at all as you imagined, or as I'd dreamed it would be before I left.

OFTEN IN THE EVENING, WHEN I WAS ALONE, I'D GO BACK over the list of goals I'd jotted down on a piece of paper when I arrived in Paris. I read the lines one by one, each line with something I wanted to change, Change my name, change my teeth, change my appearance, change my laughter. I drew tiny crosses next to the goals I considered accomplished, and promised myself that soon the metamorphosis would be complete.

The most urgent thing was to transform my teeth. That was the part of me that elicited the greatest number of questions and linked me the most to my childhood. Most of my teeth were crooked, it's true, even you made fun of them, and in Paris people asked me why they were so badly skewed.

Once again it was Ludovic who helped me. He took me to lunch in a restaurant in the Faubourg Saint-Honoré, one of the richest neighborhoods of Paris. When we arrived men and women took our coats, accompanied us to our table and pulled out the chairs for us to sit down. They served us drinks from a little wooden trolley with silver trim, and when we left Ludovic gave them a banknote as a tip. A banknote.

I know you'd have disapproved of that kind of place— I was fascinated. But to come back to what I was saying, Ludovic was talking, he said something and I smiled. It was when I looked down and my smile revealed my teeth under my lips that he said in the softest possible voice, clearly trying not to hurt my feelings, You know, I really think you should do something about your teeth. You're a good-looking guy, it's a pity to have such bad teeth. Once again I felt the shame burn inside me. His kindness couldn't efface it, Elena, as if shame was an objective feeling, inscribed in the very matter of the world, on which individual wills had no hold or effect, as if nothing, neither kindness nor delicacy, nor pride, nor the processes of history and popular uprisings could have any bearing on what the world has forever chosen to mark with shame: poverty, ugliness, abjection. And you know if you want to get by in Paris, Ludovic continued—I can still remember the lull in his voice—having teeth like that gives you a kind of northern air, if you see what I mean.

It was like the day when you taught me how to hold my knife and fork, I didn't say anything. I'd learned to keep silent. I smiled to hide my shame while doing my best not to open my mouth. Ludovic signaled to the waiter that he wanted the bill. The waiter came over in silence. Ludovic took his wallet from his inside jacket pocket, opened it to take out his American Express card and said Would you let me make an appointment for you at a dental clinic? They'll take care of your problem, you won't have to pay a thing. I nodded, Yes, yes, I'd love that.

Shame ran down my face, but I was happy, if you only knew how that shook me to the core.

The next week I was sitting in the waiting room, with a thick red carpet under my feet and art on the walls. The secretary offered me a glass of water, I nodded and looked around the room. Everything gave the impression of luxury, I wished you could have seen it, everything was meant to remind the patients of their wealth and importance. I followed the dentist when she called me but walking behind her I felt the fear rise in my body. The complexes about my class and origins that I was able to overcome most of the time came rushing back; I knew that in other contexts I could play a role, pretend that I was someone else or even lie about my past, but this woman was taking me down the hall to a room where she'd examine my body, and my body was the hardest part of me to control, the one I couldn't force to lie, the concrete materialization of my past, my past made blood, flesh and bone.

I lay back in the chair and when she looked inside my mouth the dentist exclaimed, Oh my, not a pretty sight! I found myself in the same situation as when your mother asked me what my parents did for a living, I felt completely blocked, and like with your mother I decided to speak as directly as possible to overcome my shame, and said I come from a family where no one has any money and nobody looks after their teeth. She raised her eyebrows, But this is France, everyone can get their teeth looked after more or less for free. She didn't wait for a response, Elena, she wouldn't let me respond, she kept sticking her fingers in my mouth and giving me instructions, Open wider, There, like that, but what she'd just said kept echoing in my mind, the shame was too strong, I had to respond to expel it, I had to give an explanation. I tried to go on. I did what I did with your mother that night, and said, Yes but you know I grew up in the north of France where everyone eats with their fingers so nobody cares about their teeth. I forced a laugh, but I was crying inside. I hated myself, I hated myself, of course I regretted it, it was shame that made me speak. Do you think I'm a bad person? The dentist didn't so much as blink, she treated several cavities then said, There are a lot, we've got our work cut out for us. She asked me to come back the following week and suggested I visit an orthodontist to see about straightening my crooked teeth.

When I left the office the secretary said that the bill had been paid. I phoned Ludovic to thank him, explained what had happened and told him what the dentist had said about seeing an orthodontist, he said I could choose the one I wanted and he'd send me a check to pay for it.

It took four years to straighten my teeth, from the time I arrived in Paris at eighteen until I was twenty-two. A week to the day after the dentist, the orthodontist reacted in the same way. When I left his office I was in so much pain that I had to take medication that dulled my mind. Headaches woke me up in the middle of the night, I'd have liked to smash my jaw against the wall to stop the pain, or at least replace it with another. And yet, I'd tell myself, this pain is proof that you're changing.

After my teeth I changed my first name in court, and then my last name. I went to a clinic to alter my hairline, I dressed in a different way, one that seemed better suited to my life.

One by one I was erasing the traces of what I'd been.

LISTEN.

I'd like to tell you how I learned to create the present, to prevent it from disappearing entirely from my life and so as not to suffocate from my obsession with metamorphosis: I walk in the night. It's summer and I'm walking in the night, slowly, because I'm hoping something will happen and I know that here, in the streets surrounding the Place de la République near Ludovic's flat, it's not entirely out of the question that something will. I was counting on the night to help me forget my struggle, my future. I knew I'd succeeded when I heard a voice behind me, "Hey!" Even before I turned around I knew I'd love him and lust after him, as if I could already hear his beauty in his voice. I didn't turn around. I wanted him to say it again. I wanted to hear the sound of his beauty once again.

I kept walking, "Hey!" he repeated, and only then did I turn around and see the eyeless face under his cap; I could only

see his jawbone and his body under his T-shirt, his powerful, compact body that tugged at the thin white fabric of his
T-shirt as if his flesh had a will of its own.

He spoke: You got a light? To light my cigarette.

I knew it was a lie. He didn't want a light, he didn't need to
light a cigarette, but I played along; I pretended to believe his
question, or rather to believe that his question was a question,
and I said Sorry I don't smoke; he let some time pass. What
our silence expressed was that he and I both knew exactly
what was going to happen, that the silence was merely the
anticipation of a future that was already certain. I watched
him search for the right words. I still hadn't seen his eyes;
I guessed at them, I invented them. Even the rest of his face I
only saw as reflections in the night. Then he said: I'm a shark.
(Silence.) Do you like sharks? (Silence again.) I laughed and
he eyed me: No? So I answered somewhere between laughter
and seriousness: Sure, I mean yes.

He smiled under his cap, and suddenly faced with his smile
I no longer found what he'd said at all funny or ridiculous, on
the contrary, it was as if I'd never heard anything so serious
or so profound. He was a shark, here in the night; I believed
him. He went on: You live far from here? I said no, and asked
if he wanted to walk with me. We walked together for five or
so minutes. When we got to the door of my building—it was
bright blue—I pressed the code; he was right behind me, I felt
his warm breath on my neck. I thought: that's the breath of
a shark. I know sharks don't have breath but I kept saying to
myself, that's the breath of a shark.

(Is it possible to write these words and thoughts? Is it possible to write them when their beauty came from the thick-

ness of the night and the charge of desire and passion that embedded them? Jean Genet says: "Erotic play discloses a nameless world which is revealed by the nocturnal language of lovers. Such language is not written down. It is whispered into the ear at night in a hoarse voice. At dawn it is forgotten." I haven't forgotten.)

I went up the stairs two at a time, he followed me, and in my flat he took off his cap. I saw his eyes for the first time. I ran my hand over his shaved head, his black hair, barely a millimeter long, scraped against my skin. I touched my lips to his neck and it was at that precise moment, when my lips brushed against the skin behind his ear, that he picked me up and laid me on the bed with a strength that was so tranquil and so self-assured that you'd have thought—I mean, seen from the outside—that he was the one who was at home and that I was the stranger he'd met in the night.

He took possession of everything, the space, the situation, my body. My face was pressed against the fabric of the mattress, my gaze plunged in darkness. I could hear the sound of his belt as he undid it, the sound of his flies, of his jeans sliding down his thighs, the warmth of his body against me. I could feel my own breath on my face; he still didn't say anything—and I swear I'd never heard such beautiful silence.

We made love several times. In between he talked to me, saying: You're going to leave with me. We're going to go far from here and stay together our whole lives.

I didn't know his name.

He whispered: You'll be my wife. You'll become my wife and you'll be mine, and I said yes, I said yes.

The next morning he left. He put his cap back on and his eyes were hidden like the day before. He left my flat without a word, I'd watched him wash in the bathroom without saying anything. I thought: maybe he regrets the words the night made him say; I looked at his back, his shoulders for the last time.

Today many years have passed, and as I share this memory with you I imagine him going off again into the night, emerging

THE STUDIO

from the shadows at random and saying to others the same words he spoke to me the night we met. I imagine the smile on the face of the one who doesn't yet understand the extent to which these words are the most beautiful, the most solemn and the most serious he will ever hear, the noblest and most sacred words that anyone will ever say to him.

I must say something: during these nighttime encounters—there were others—the past and the future disappeared. I was no longer afraid. All of my fears, about my future, my metamorphosis, the shadows of the past, Amiens, you, all of that, dissolved in the night. These encounters were the only times when I lived in the reality we call the present.*

---

* One day one of these encounters almost killed me, but that's another story.

WHAT DID I WANT IN PARIS, DEEP DOWN? EVEN TODAY IT'S not clear to me. Did I want to become bourgeois? to get rich? to become an intellectual? to be famous? to be rid of the threat of poverty for good? was it above all change that I wanted, or change in the sense of social climbing? It strikes me that it was all these things at once, I think that my desires evolved according to the context, situation, and people I was with.

What is certain is that since I'd given up writing I asked myself more and more questions, I was afraid. What would become of me? I could have told myself that I was living in Paris and studying at a prestigious university, I could count on having a well-paid job and a place in the world of the privileged, but that wasn't enough. My body demanded more, Elena, the violence of the first years of my life required greater compensation, I had no choice, my body—that is, the superposition of all my accumulated experiences—demanded that I go further.

I sought help. I've forgotten how I came up with the idea, but it struck me that if I wasn't able to get by on my own through writing, I'd have to meet someone who'd take me into his life, someone through whom I'd take revenge on the past. He'd have to be a millionaire, a prince, an important politician, no matter, but the life he would reveal to me had to be equal to my need for revenge.

[Don't judge me, I'm simply trying to be as honest with you as I can.]

The day I met the heir of a family that was so grand, so time-honored that we'd learned about it at school, you and I, in a course on the birth of European industrialization in the nineteenth century, I did everything I could to see him again, to charm him and to get him to like me. I invited him to come and spend time in Ludovic's little studio, to go for walks with me in the afternoon. I wanted so much to be like him, to be part of his reality. He had the accent of the French upper classes, his mouth almost stayed closed when he talked. I envied him. I imitated him. I'd have given anything to be him and to swap my life for his. I didn't like him, something in me couldn't like him, my past, my experience of the world, but I persisted. I forced myself. I told myself that my feelings were secondary, that the key thing was to save myself.

After him there was Manuel, whom I met in Barcelona. I'd gone there on a cheap flight, and with a room in a kind of hostel costing twenty euros a night the whole weekend set me back less than a hundred euros. I only had enough money to buy half-baguettes for twenty cents apiece in the supermarket, which I ate sitting on a bench near Las Ramblas avenue, but I was happy to be in another country.

The evening I saw Manuel for the first time I chatted with him and after a few minutes he told me that he was the mayor of Geneva. I clutched on to that encounter and didn't let go. [Don't judge me.] I wrote to him regularly, I went to see him in Switzerland once a month. He lived in a big house in the mountains on the edge of Geneva, every day there was a woman who cleaned the house, made me coffee when I woke up, and ironed my clothes. It was even more than I'd bargained for. I swam in his pool in the garden behind his house, surrounded by trees and rosebushes. He invited me to the Locarno Film Festival, and when night fell I had dinner with important people Manuel introduced me to, actresses, bankers, the mayor of Zurich. I said Manuel was my father. I asked him to adopt me, he hesitated, I insisted. If he'd accepted I'd have taken metamorphosis to new heights by even choosing my own father. I repeated my request at every opportunity, in the swimming pool during the day or in big Geneva hotels in the evening. When I got back to Paris and people asked me what my father did—in fact I'd find ways of bringing it up even when I wasn't asked—I'd say: he's the mayor of Geneva, and I felt strong, important. (Manuel is the only person from this phase of my life I'm still friends with, with whom I share a true friendship. He wasn't like the others, he was funny, generous, intelligent, sensitive.)

I didn't stop after Manuel (he didn't want to adopt me), and did all I could to meet other people. I can't describe them all to you, there was the creator of a line of cosmetics who lived in Los Angeles, whom I'd met on that weekend in Barcelona and who would invite me to join him in Spain after that, often for a few days, his secretary would send me the plane ticket, he'd travel from Los Angeles to Barcelona to be with me. As with the heir to the industrialist family I didn't like him but I tried not to think about it. I had to escape, escape, escape.

Did I tell you about the man with the sofa? He was the one who contacted me, on an online chat forum. He was the president of one of the biggest banks in the United States; I searched the name of the bank on Google and sure enough it was true, his picture appeared, there on the page, his name was mentioned in the world's biggest newspapers. I was already envisaging a life with him, moving to America, infinite wealth—as always the same words resonating in my head, Thanks to him I'll be saved. He invited me to a restaurant on the Champs-Élysées, and after dinner I went with him to his place. I'd never seen such a big, impressive apartment, like a glass mansion suspended over one of the most beautiful streets in Paris. He gave me a glass of red wine, no doubt the bottle cost several hundred euros, and told me about the grape variety and vintage. I could follow what he was saying, at night I'd been reading up on wine on the Internet, I studied it the way you'd study at school, the difference between Bordeaux and Burgundies, the greatest wine estates, the differences between first and second labels, I had to know all of that for my new life, and in fact when these men saw how much I knew about wine I could see the admiration in their eyes. My nights of studying paid off. It's because my father's the mayor of Geneva and he's always loved good wine, I'd say nonchalantly. [Don't judge me.]

That evening I looked out at the city through the huge bay

windows, as if I was floating above Paris. The bank president gently placed a record on the record player, the music started, and with my glass in my hand and the music in my ears, I thought of my childhood, of the village. I thought of you.

Tapping beside him on the white sofa and motioning to me to come over, he said *Come and sit with me*, and I joined him. When I was about to sit down he said *Careful, don't spill your wine on the sofa, it's polar bear.* His sofa was covered with polar bear fur. I flinched but said nothing. I stifled my disgust, and clinked glasses with him.

For the time being I kept my disgust and indignation under wraps. I was too weak to let them get the better of me, it's only now that I allow myself to think what I'm describing to you. Questioning the violence of the world was not a luxury I could afford, the key thing was to keep going. After the evening at the bank president's (I never saw him again, I'd like to tell you that it was me who decided not to see him anymore, but he was the one who didn't contact me), my money problems accumulated. It happened quite suddenly. I was working as an usher at the Théâtre de l'Odéon, I had the same job as at the Maison de la Culture in Amiens but I was only a substitute and some months I didn't earn any money at all. I kept going to the dentist and the orthodontist once or twice a month, and the whole treatment spread over four years cost several thousand euros. Ludovic wasn't paying the bills anymore, no doubt he had other things on his mind, and I didn't dare to bring it up. I was left with no money, and debts to pay.

I often had dinner with him, or with Didier, they asked me out, but other nights I didn't always manage to eat, I went from evenings in luxurious restaurants with Ludovic or brasseries frequented by artists and intellectuals with Didier to others when I didn't eat a thing, in the space of twenty-four hours my reality swung from one extreme to the other. I'd cook pasta for dinner and reheat it the next day, the leftover pasta was dry and starchy, my stomach would heave when I ate it. I learned to get by on just one meal a day to save money, a habit that has stuck with me ever since.

The hardest thing was telling the dentist that I couldn't afford to pay, my shame when I asked if I could pay later. Money was becoming an obsession, Elena, I'd go to bed thinking about it, when I woke up the next morning it was the first thing on my mind. I'd heard about a way to earn a lot, easily and quickly. I decided that it was what I'd have to do; I visited dating sites and started seeing men whom I'd sleep with for money. Even though it didn't go well the first time I kept going and offered to meet other men, it was the job that seemed the least trying, the least humiliating and the least alienating, at least less so than working as a waiter or a dishwasher in a restaurant for a miserable salary. I looked for men on dating sites but stopped short of registering on professional escort services; I don't know why but I hesitated to take that step, then with time it became more difficult to find takers, those who were really ready to pay and who were willing to pay the most used specialized websites, not just simple dating sites.

I had to collect my thoughts and come up with other ways of earning money, I worked as a secretary in a law firm, a guinea pig for medical students, a French tutor, a caretaker.

One afternoon when I was on duty, my supervisor led me to a concrete courtyard and told me to clean it with a pressure washer. I'd never used one before and hurt my leg testing the water flow, the pressure was so strong that it stripped away the skin. I was wearing a tattered old pair of tracksuit bottoms, and as I scrubbed with a broom after spraying the walls and floor I started to cry. There in that courtyard I was sure I'd failed, and all my efforts had been for nothing, I thought of Amiens and my struggle to get to Paris, my years of battling with my body, with my habits, with the school system, my failures and recoveries, my new ways of eating, talking, laughing, my new clothes, and it was all for nothing, my destiny had caught up with me, I was scrubbing the floor of a building belonging to rich people. I sat on the soaked floor and didn't move, paralyzed by my defeat.

It was through Didier that I found what struck me as a way out. He was presenting and signing his new book in a bookshop, Les Cahiers de Colette. I'd arrived a few minutes early, it wasn't the first time I'd been to an event like this, and even though I'd dropped my attempts at writing I viewed Didier with a mixture of envy and fascination. I advanced between the shelves amid the smell of paper, and Didier introduced me to Colette, the woman who'd created the bookshop and given it its name. After the signing we talked and she said that I could come and work for her if I wanted, she needed someone starting the following week. Didier must have told her about me, she acted like someone who was trying to protect me.

I said yes, and she asked me to come by the following Tuesday. That's how I became a bookseller (I didn't work

there every day of course, only on the days I had no classes).
It was more difficult than I'd imagined, contrary to my expectations it didn't just involve recommending books and
discussing them with customers, you also had to lug boxes,
take out the books, sort them, stack them on the shelves, and
store the ones that had been there for too long without being sold; but I could also read the books I wanted, and every
day I discovered new authors when customers asked for them,
Vladimir Nabokov, Emily Dickinson, Peter Handke. I read
on my lunch break, and in the quieter hours when there were
no customers. Didier had told me that Colette's bookshop had
a huge reputation and was frequented by well-known artists,
authors and politicians; I watched them from the storeroom
where I was sorting books but didn't dare speak to them—
until the day Philippe came in. I heard him say to Colette,
Who's the angel in the corner? Colette replied that my name
was Édouard. He came up to me, I smiled and we talked.
Before he left he gave me his phone number and said he'd like
to see me again.

(I FORGOT TO SAY, THE DAY AFTER MY EVENING WITH THE man with the polar bear sofa, almost by coincidence I'd gone to see my father in the small town in the Nord department where he still lives. I hadn't seen him for a long time, a couple of years. I walked through the quiet, lifeless streets from the train station to the little council flat he'd just moved into. The tower blocks were gray and cold and the stairwells smelled of urine, my father complained about it when I arrived.

The moment he opened the door of his flat and I saw him and the poverty that saturated every inch of the place where he was living, the smell of fried food, the huge TV screen in front of the table where he ate, his body destroyed by a life of misery and exclusion, I thought of the man from the night before and his polar bear sofa, I thought of his wines worth hundreds of euros, and language failed me. I couldn't find anything inside me to measure this distance, the ugliness and violence of the world. I don't know what it was, this storm inside my body, the anger, the despair, the disgust, even my feelings had no name. I knew that if I tried to explain this gap back in Paris no one would understand it, I couldn't have expressed it because it's outside of language. I knew that if language was powerless then I shouldn't try to convince these people, the ones in my new life, but fight them. Maybe it was that afternoon in front of my father that I promised myself I'd avenge him one day.)

THE DAY PHILIPPE GAVE ME HIS PHONE NUMBER, ONCE again I couldn't help thinking: I've succeeded, or rather, *I've made it*. I had the feeling that in getting close to him I was making up for all the failures of the past months, all the encounters that had come to nothing, and the more I saw him the stronger that feeling became. In the evenings he'd invite me to restaurants where my only thought was that the child I'd been could never have imagined that such places existed. These restaurants had nothing in common with the ones Ludovic and Didier took me to, not even with the ones I'd been to with Manuel, it was as if they were less places for eating than for reassuring guests of their importance, as if the very word restaurant out front was a lie. Systematically when we arrived, a man in a chauffeur's hat would take Philippe's car and park it for him. Philippe would enter the dining hall and another person, usually a woman, would whisk our coats away to the cloakroom while yet another would escort us to our table. When Philippe asked about wine the waiter would send for the sommelier, who'd tell us about the wines on the list as if he was talking about rare treasures. I read the unimaginable prices of the bottles printed on the menu Philippe was holding, but I wasn't yet suffering from this injustice. As with the man and his sofa I wasn't yet suffering from the scandalous gap between my new life and my old one. Even though I'd seen my father not long before, I stifled my questions and my pain and lived in the intoxication of my metamorphosis (and as with Ludovic, it was clear that what pushed Philippe to help me was desire).

Philippe introduced me to his world, where the aristocracy mixed with the fabulously wealthy. During the several months

Aquitaine caviar, celery root espuma on toast

Fillet of John Dory, samphire risotto
Sea urchin coral butter

Selection of cheeses

Red fruit and vanilla cream

Coffee
Mignardises

Domaine de Grandmaison 2009 "Pessac-Léognan"

Château Chasse-Spleen 2006 "Moulis-en-Médoc"

I spent with him, he invited me to evening get-togethers where I met dukes and princesses, aristocrats who had often converted to the art trade or other fields. When I left my body to observe myself, as I'd done at parties when I'd arrived in Paris, I told myself that I'd achieved my dream. I'd escaped, I'd come further than I could ever have hoped. I imagined Philippe doing what I'd been waiting for all this time: asking me to live with him and forever putting myself and my past far behind me.

During the week he'd take me to receptions at the Automobile Club, I don't know quite how to explain to you what that is, a sort of association of the rich and powerful who get together to eat caviar, drink champagne and forge ties. I rubbed shoulders with ministers and members of parliament, millionaires and presidents of multinationals; on Mondays—the day they were closed—I went with Philippe to museums that people travel thousands of miles and cross continents to visit. The Louvre, the Musée d'Orsay, Philippe and I and ten or so others had them entirely to ourselves. I talked with princesses and felt like I was part of their world—I didn't even know that princesses still existed in real life. I remember a woman who introduced herself as the Princesse de Broglie, and how I'd laughed to myself because—do you remember?—I'd had to read a text on the Broglie family in a course on the Ancien Régime when we were at the lycée or university. I'd pronounced the name BROGLIE and the teacher had corrected me, saying you don't say Broglie but "Breuil," it's spelled Broglie but pronounced Breuil. Now I was joking with the descendants of this dynasty, that thrilled me to no end. I'd go to dinners where I was seated beside Philippe at huge tables covered with flowers and candlesticks, in front of me a plate with dozens of different knives and forks, I had no idea which ones to use, so I waited to see how the others did it. One evening, one of the first times, Philippe had whispered in my ear *I hope you like caviar, it's on the menu tonight.*

Yes, sure I do, I answered, I didn't admit to him that I'd never tasted it, I don't know if he saw that. He smiled his usual playful smile and added, Anyway, keep the menu, each one's unique, maybe in ten years you can sell it and become rich.

I was sure I'd reached the summit of the world, Elena. I wrote to you less and less, our bodies were moving apart, not so much in time—I'd been in Paris for just over a year, not so long—as, in a way, in social space. I remember replying to one of your messages one evening while waiting for Philippe in the street, saying I was busy and I'd write later. Can I turn back time? Will you forgive me? Philippe had arranged to meet me in front of a large building with a sculpted facade

between the National Assembly and Saint-Germain-des-Prés. I was wearing a fitted navy-blue jacket and matching trousers, with a white shirt and tie. I'd looked at myself in the mirror for a long time before leaving home, the Windsor knot visible in the opening of the jacket I'd bought thanks to money Philippe had sent me. Before joining him I'd scrutinized the person in the mirror and thought: *You've come far.* I'd walked through Paris, proud of my appearance, holding a bottle of wine that I'd bought along the way. Philippe arrived and apologized for being late. He complimented me on my tie, asked me what I had in my hand and when he saw the bottle he told me that there was no need, he'd bought one as a gift from both of us. All the better, I said, then we'll have two bottles instead of one, but I felt he was mildly embarrassed, piqued even. I understood that the bottle I'd bought wasn't good enough for his friends. I pretended to laugh, I had an idea, I'd leave the bottle in the street, someone would pick it up as they walked by, but Philippe retorted that I couldn't just leave a bottle in the street. Put it in your bag and drink it with your friends this week, he said.

I didn't try to gainsay him again.

Philippe rang at the front gate, we walked up the stairs and a woman dressed entirely in black opened the door. I followed Philippe into the apartment—not so much an apartment as a house concealed inside a Parisian building. The rooms stretched out before my eyes and under my feet, stairs led to the upper floors. Philippe showed me the paintings on the walls, saying: Kandinsky, Cocteau, and: this is a sketch by Picasso. I'm not sure of the names anymore, but I'm sure he said names that impressed me, names so famous that I'd known them since I was a child. I asked with a cocky air: How much does a painting like that cost? Philippe smiled: So much it makes no sense to ask.

It was to experience scenes like these that I left you—but I had the right, it seems to me I had the right.

I remember many such soirées in Philippe's world. The people around him would talk about the opera, the trips they'd taken, I'll never forget the man who exclaimed: *I must say I much prefer the beaches of Southeast Asia to those in California! Asia is so much more authentic.* I felt reasonably comfortable, especially when it came to music. As I've told you I used to go to the opera with Didier and Geoffroy, and after that with Philippe. I could talk about Massenet, I compared Wagner with Shostakovich, knowing about the opera gave me confidence. I'd try to say things that would make me look good, I think Massenet is vastly underestimated, or In my view Mozart's works for the opera die on the vine, such phrases flowed from my mouth. I hid my distaste for the fatty foods that were served at these parties, the hare *à la royale*, for instance, a nauseating overkill of meats, or for the sheer quantity of food, the platters of cheese served after dishes that were already rich, all of which I later allowed myself to see as marks of the vulgarity of the rich. Philippe was proud to have me with him, I'd always mention that I was studying at the École Normale Supérieure, without specifying that I'd got in through the least prestigious admissions procedure, that I was bogus, an intruder.

A last image from that life. One evening a woman who worked for some friends of Philippe's was helping me to salad to go with the cheese tray and the Bordeaux—Chasse-Spleen, Philippe's favorite. She was standing just behind me and preparing to serve me when the spoons slipped through her fingers and fell into the metal bowl with a clatter. The man who lived there, our host, Philippe's friend, stopped what he was saying and turned to her: For goodness' sake, Katia, watch what you're doing. Then to the others: She's so frightfully clumsy, it's the same thing week in, week out. She was standing there, right next to us, a few inches away, she could hear him but he was talking about her in the third person, as if she weren't there, as if her reaction and her feelings were so unimportant that she didn't deserve that he wait until she'd left the room. His words pierced my flesh. I wanted to stand up and tell this woman that I wasn't like them, that I was not on their side, but I kept silent.

Later I told Didier about this dinner and said I'd defended Katia in front of the others but it wasn't true. I lied because I was ashamed that I hadn't said anything, I hoped my lie would prove that I still knew how to be ashamed, and that I was a decent person. I'd like Didier to know I'm ashamed of not telling him I remained silent.

And I want you to know as well.

IV

DENOUEMENT

FAILURE

ONE DAY THIS LIFE WITH PHILIPPE CAME TO AN END. IT had lasted for several months, during which I believed I'd put my childhood and my fears behind me.

There's nothing particular to tell, no sudden breakup or argument that would stick in my mind, one day it ended, that's all.

Now that I'd tried this life, was I weary of it? Had I understood that I'd never fit into this world? Did I convince myself I had to leave it, so as not to be confronted with the fact that it would have nothing to do with me, that we were radically incompatible? Or was it, quite simply, that this life and these people repelled me, and that I thought to myself I didn't want to be like them? I think it's mostly that, but I don't know, I hate to favor this reason as it's the noblest and most flattering (and yet I really do believe it, I remember thinking that I hated not Philippe but those evenings with him).

I think this was at the beginning of 2012. After the breakup I got closer to Didier and Geoffroy again. I went on holiday with them, we went out more and more, to the theater, the cinema, the opera, they introduced me to an intellectual, artistic world. With them was born one of the most beautiful friendships in history, I'm sure (but I never forgot Elena). I wrote short articles on novels and essays in a gay magazine, thanks to Didier who'd recommended me to the editor, I practiced putting texts together, I wanted to begin all over again, to start from scratch with the dream that had brought me to Paris. I organized meetings on sociology and literature at the Théâtre de l'Odéon, I saw my name printed on the programs and felt that I existed in the eyes of others, I felt reborn.

Now I was sure I had to write a book, that was how I would save myself for good. Ludovic—whom I'd been ashamed to tell anything but a few details about the nights I'd spent with Philippe—encouraged me, he bought me books.

I had to start again, to put it all in order.

I picked up where I'd left off before meeting Philippe. Every morning I'd sit down in front of the computer to write, I'd force myself, I'd pace up and down in the tiny flat, I'd tell myself You have to do it, you have to do it, but for all the encouragement, no words came.

I'd go to cafés and jot down sentences in a little notebook, I'd try my hand at a rough draft, but everything I wrote discouraged me even more, when I reread the next day what I'd written the day before I felt sullied and ridiculed by myself, everything I wrote resembled a failed plagiarism of the authors I loved, I deleted everything, despair prevented me from going on.

BARCELONA

THEN CAME THE FINAL ABANDONMENT. EXHAUSTED from the struggle with writing, I wasted hours on social media doing nothing, saying nothing, talking to strangers, weighed down by the heaviness of my failure. I was chatting on Facebook with a man I didn't know, who lived in Barcelona. He was one of the last of a noble lineage, he'd been alone for several years and was suffering from his loneliness. I comforted him, and opened up my heart to him as well, about my escape from Amiens, my life with Philippe, my doubts. Other days I'd send him poems I was writing, attempts at poems. He told me that he had very strong feelings for me and that it must sound immature for him to say it because he was almost sixty—three times my age—but he couldn't help himself, he was falling in love.

One afternoon when he—Éric, that was his name—phoned me, I offered to come and live with him in Spain, to start all over with him there.

He said yes, right away. I resolved to leave three days later

and abandon everything, my life, my friends, my studies, the
dreams I'd formulated in Amiens with Elena, and the ones
born of my encounter with Didier. I hadn't told Éric why I
wanted to join him: because I was exhausted, because of the
extreme fatigue that comes with becoming and metamorphosis, because I'd failed.

For the three days before I left for Barcelona I pretended
to live normally. I didn't tell anyone. I saw Ludovic, Didier
and Geoffroy, I went to classes at the École Normale, I pho-
tographed everything. I wanted to retain everything I saw, all
the images and faces, and store them forever in my memory,
one last time.

I'd have liked to be able to tell the others that I was sorry,
that I had to leave because I didn't have the strength to keep
on struggling, that I was going to lose them but if I didn't
leave I'd lose everything.

The day before my flight I told Didier and Geoffroy that
we'd see each other later in the week but I knew it wasn't true.
It was a lie because I was saying see you later but I should have
said farewell.

I did say farewell but I said it to myself in silence, to
Philippe, to Didier and Geoffroy, to the years of relentless-
ness, to Elena's Windsor knot, to the sessions in front of the
mirror trying to create another laugh, to the obsession with
becoming, to dreams.

In the arrivals hall at the airport I recognized Éric, who
was waiting for me. He was smiling. He didn't look like the

pictures I'd seen of him. It wasn't that he'd lied or sent me pictures that made him look better than he did, but the reality of his body—and his body in motion—revealed something the pictures didn't show.

I looked at him and thought: *This is your new life, it's him.* He kissed me on the cheek and helped me carry my suitcase. He took me to his place, I remember his first sentence: *Welcome to our home.* He came up to kiss me and caress my body under my polo shirt, I kissed him back but I didn't like how he smelled, I hadn't thought about that when I'd talked to him on the Internet. I told him we'd make love later, that for now I was really quite shaken up at having changed my life so totally and suddenly and he said *Yes, of course I understand.*

In the evening he took me to dinner in a restaurant on Las Ramblas. He showed me his neighborhood, his favorite café, the path where he walked his dog in the morning when he woke up. He showed me these things as landmarks of our future life.

In the morning after getting up I'd go walking on the beach. The sea in front of me, the sun that warmed my skin, I stored it all as the data of my new beginning. I wandered the streets at random, trying to identify the places that would become my hangouts, the cafés where I'd go to read during the day, the pool I'd swim in in the afternoon, the quietest areas on the beach. It was March, tourists were still scarce although it was already hot out. Geoffroy wrote asking how I was doing, as he did every morning, and I replied that I was fine, as if I were still at home in Paris. The next few days I told him I was ill and couldn't leave my flat; I put off telling him that I'd left. I continued my life in Barcelona, during the day I'd tell Éric that I needed to walk alone and in the evening I'd meet him for dinner, but our conversations became more and more laborious, the silences increasingly heavy. I tried to convince myself it was normal, that this was the beginning and we needed time. *At least here you can rest, here the war is over, you no longer have to become, you just have to be*, I told myself. In the evening, when it was time to go to sleep, I'd lie in Éric's bed, staying as far as possible from his smell of cleansing milk and old leather, he'd crawl over to me and touch me and try to kiss me, I'd push him away gently, telling him I wasn't ready yet.

Things continued like that for a week, for a week I forced myself, then I told Éric that I had to go back to Paris. He didn't try to stop me, I understand, he said. I'd botched my escape.

I took the plane and when I got back to Paris I sent a few messages to Éric, then fewer and fewer. I wrote again to Didier and Geoffroy saying that I'd been ill with a high fever for several days, and was looking forward to seeing them.

RETURN AND LAST ATTEMPT

I RETURNED TO PARIS AND LUDOVIC'S FLAT, WHICH JUST over a week earlier I thought I'd left for good. Nothing had changed. All I could do was try to buckle down and work. I sat at the little table and started to write:

> My mother would spend a lot of time telling me stories about various episodes from her life or my father's.
>
> She found her own life boring and she spoke to me as a way of filling the void of her existence, which was no more than a series of boring moments and exhausting forms of work. For a long time she was a *stay-at-home mother*, as she would have me write for her on official forms. She felt insulted, sullied by the fact that my birth certificate said *none* on the line for mother's occupation. When my younger brother and sister were old enough to take care of themselves, she wanted to get a job. My father found the idea demeaning, as if it would call his masculinity into question; he was the one who should be bringing home the paycheck. It was something

she had a fierce desire to do, no matter that the only lines of work open to her were hard: the factory, housework, or working the register at a supermarket. She fought for what she wanted. In a way, she was also struggling against herself, against an elusive, unnameable force that encouraged her to think it was degrading for a woman to work when her husband had been forced into unemployment. (My father had lost his job at the factory, I'll come back to this.) After much discussion, my father finally agreed and she began working as a home aide helping elderly people bathe, getting around the village from house to house on her rusty bicycle, wearing a red parka of my father's from a few years back, now moth-eaten and of course (given my father's size) too big for her. The other women of the village laughed at the sight *Look how stylish she is, that Mrs. Bellegueule, in her great big parka.* When on one occasion it turned out that she had earned more than my father, a bit more than a thousand euros for her and a bit less than seven hundred for him, he couldn't take it anymore. He told her there was no point and that she should quit, that we didn't need the extra money. Seven hundred euros for seven of us would be enough.

I was writing down all of my childhood, the past against which I'd struggled, my mother's words, everything that had pushed me to leave for Amiens and start my metamorphosis, everything that had been at the root of my despair and anger, the words and sentences and memories came back to me, I typed them on the keyboard and the next day I reworked what I'd written the day before, I worked seven, eight hours a day; I wrote and the more I advanced the more I thought that this book would be what would save me; in a strange, brutal reversal I wrote to describe what I'd been struggling to hide for so many years; recalling it now I wrote:

My father. In 1967, the year he was born, women from the village didn't yet go to the hospital. They gave birth at home. When she had my father, his mother was lying on a dirty sofa covered in cat and dog hair along with the dirt from shoes constantly caked with mud and never taken off at the door. There are, of course, paved roads in the village, but also *trails* that are still heavily used, where children go to play, tracks made of dirt and unpaved stone that run alongside fields, paths of beaten-down earth that become like quicksand when it rains.

Before I started middle school, I would go out several times a week to ride my bicycle on these *trails*. I'd attach a little piece of cardboard to the spokes of my bike so that it would make the sound of a motorbike as I pedaled.

My father's father drank heavily, pastis and wine from five-liter boxes, as is usual for most men in the village. It's the alcohol found at the grocery store, which also serves as a café and a place to buy cigarettes and bread. You can buy anything at any time of day, by just knocking on the owners' door. They'll always help you out.

His father drank heavily and, once drunk, would beat my grandmother: he would turn toward her all of a sudden and start insulting her, throwing anything he could reach at her, even his chair sometimes, and then he would beat her. My father, small as he was, trapped in the body of a scrawny child, watched them, helpless. He stored up his hate in silence.

He never told me any of this. My father never spoke, at least about those kinds of things. My mother took that on as part of what women were supposed to do.

One morning—my father was five years old—his father left for good, with no warning. My grandmother, another keeper of the family history (again the role of women), told me about this event. It would make her laugh years later, happy, finally, to have got free from her husband *Left for work at the factory one morning and never came home for supper, we waited.* He was a factory worker, he brought the money into the house, and when he disappeared the family found itself broke, with barely enough to eat for six or seven children.

My father never forgot, saying in front of me *That fucking son of a bitch who abandoned us, left my mother with nothing, I'd piss all over him if I had the chance.*

THE END

I WORKED AT THAT RHYTHM FOR SEVERAL MONTHS. I'D wake up, and start to write. I didn't eat during the day. I promised myself that I'd get some rest: once I'd published the book and it had avenged me for the past I could retire forever, never do anything again. In the evenings and at night I read as much as possible, dozens of novels, to stimulate my memory, the real or imagined memories of the writers I read paved the way for memories of my own, I read to learn how to remember. I read at night, but also on the metro on the way to university, at lunchtime between classes, in the evening. I had no time to lose, I even listened to audiobooks in the shower. I bought or stole books and stacked them in the flat, there were books on the floor, in the sink, on the shelf in the bathroom. I'd count: Two or so years ago you hadn't read a thing and now you've read between two hundred and three hundred books, keep going, keep going, I'd spur myself on, in a year you'll have read two hundred more, keep at it and in two years you'll have read another four hundred.

I feel so far removed from writers who describe how they discovered literature through their love of words and fascination with a poetic vision of the world. I'm not like them. I wrote to exist.

In the evenings when I was with Ludovic I'd talk to him about my dreams, *maybe if I can write and publish a novel I'll be known around the world, maybe if my book is read all over the world I'll be saved from poverty once and for all, I'll buy a flat, that's the first thing I'll do, I'll buy a flat and I'll be safe for the rest of my life, I'll never be homeless.* I'd print out the chapters I'd written, reread them, rewrite them, retype them on the computer, and start again. Often I stopped believing in it for days on end, melancholy, the same melancholy that had pushed me to leave for Barcelona, invaded all the niches of my life, the food I ate wasn't as good because I wasn't able to write, the wine Geoffroy gave me at his place wasn't as tasty because I wasn't able to write, Paris was more stifling because I knew I'd never make it, my whole perception of reality, all of my senses, my whole body was conditioned by the possibility of writing; Ludovic was worried and so were Geoffroy and Didier, they advised me to see a doctor, he prescribed stronger doses of antidepressants, my whole body ached.

I continued until the day when, after dozens of successive periods of despondency, the book was finished. I printed it. I reread it again, I'd reread and rewritten the sentences so many times that I knew them by heart. I gave a copy of the manuscript to Didier and Geoffroy and one to Ludovic, they read it and suggested some changes, I reworked the text one last time with their advice in mind and sent the final version to several publishers whose addresses I'd found on the Internet.

I'd called the book *Life and Death of Eddy Bellegueule*, later the title changed to *The End of Eddy*. I attached a letter to the manuscript explaining that the book was the story of my childhood.

I waited.

At first I received negative responses from the publishers. They said that nobody could believe what I'd written—though in fact all I'd done was tell scenes from my childhood. It's strange, these publishers were so far removed from what I'd described that they thought such a reality doesn't exist, that the child I'd been had never existed, so much poverty and violence couldn't exist in France, they said.

More rejections came in, but one afternoon a man called me. His name was René, he was an editor at the Seuil publishing house, he told me that he'd read my book and that it had overwhelmed him, that's the word he used, overwhelmed, I repeated it to myself for weeks afterward. I was sitting on the sofa, holding back my tears. He explained to me that he needed the approval of the publishing house but that he was sure, he'd publish my book the following year. I hung up, I couldn't hold it in any longer, I was crying, I called Didier and Geoffroy to tell them.

I left the flat and ran to join them and celebrate, it was cold out but I didn't feel the cold on my skin, I ran and thought: You're saved now, you're saved forever, you've made it.

The streets around me became distorted by the tears in my eyes and silently, under my skin, I said goodbye to the past.

EPILOGUE

MY WHOLE LIFE CHANGED AFTER THE PUBLICATION OF that book and the others I wrote after it. It's strange, the things I dreamed and fantasized about on those evenings when I talked with Ludovic and wasn't even sure I'd finish my first book came true, as if facts and reality had submitted to my will.

Suddenly what I wrote was being translated, in Italy, in China, in Greece, I traveled the world, I toured Japan presenting my work—what I now called my work—I saw Chile, Kosovo, Argentina, Norway. It was like yet another step in my metamorphosis, as if this new life had been added to the one in the village, the one in Amiens and the one in Paris, like an extra degree of reality. Newspapers and TV stations all over the world asked me questions, the dream of the little boy I'd been had come true, I'd have liked to travel back in time to tell him that everything would be all right, that he shouldn't be afraid. I'd have liked to tell him that one day he would finally exist, that certain people would consider him worthy of the attention of others, that he'd be invited to talk in places whose names he didn't yet know.

I earned money, I was able to buy a flat in Paris as I'd dreamed of doing, a flat that would keep me safe for the rest of my life and keep me off the street. With this money I was also able to travel, to America, to Southeast Asia, I discovered civilizations other than my own.

As time went by I began to sincerely love art and literature, I no longer wrote just to get by but for literature itself, not to save myself but to try to help others, maybe it's banal to put it like that but it's true, I wanted to write books that would arm others for their struggles. I distanced myself for good from my childhood, from Eddy Bellegueule.

One day I ran away (again). After my books were published, one afternoon I left for the United States, I didn't tell anyone. I packed my bag and set off because all of a sudden I hated what my life had become: the life I'd dreamed of, the life of books. I'd expected such happiness as an author and I hadn't found it, I resented my life because it had betrayed me and lied to me by not giving me what it had dangled in front of me. I went to live on another continent, I traveled for months across the States, I walked through deserted, ghostly cities, I strode alone at night through cities I didn't know and where no one knew me, I slept in random, seedy hotels, and thought: It's all starting over. The village, Amiens, Paris, New York and now New Bedford, Massachusetts, where I was celebrating my twenty-fifth birthday alone, not knowing what the future would hold, where everything could begin once again, where I'd given myself a new name, new dreams of silence and disappearance, new expectations, where for me the most beautiful thing was to lose everything I'd struggled so hard to gain in Paris. After a few months I returned to France, already weary.

Am I doomed always to hope for another life?

I write because I think that sometimes I regret having distanced myself from the past, sometimes I'm not sure that my efforts came to anything. Sometimes I think that the whole struggle was in vain, and that in escaping I fought for a happiness I never obtained.

I write because I often think I'd like to go back in time to when I spent my evenings at the bus stop with the other youngsters in the village, drinking whisky we'd bought at the supermarket from plastic cups until three or four in the morning, like the last generation of youngsters had done before us, like my brother and my father did before me, without thinking about the future or the world to come.

I'd like to go back . . .

To the times when changing wasn't a matter of urgency for me, when I went with the neighbor's children or my best friend Amélie to the wheat fields that surrounded the village and built wooden shacks with boards we'd got at the village dump and loaded on our bikes—and the smell of the wood, the earth, the rusty nails, that stayed on my fingers for days, and the damp nights we spent pretending we were comfortable when our backs ached and we were cold but happy to sleep in these shacks we'd built with our own hands, our own creations.

––––––

(It's the present that I miss.)

To the times when my father watched horror films at night and would force me to watch them with him, saying it would toughen me up. I'd tell him I wanted to go to bed but he'd order me to stay in the living room and watch the film, he'd threaten me and tell me that I had to learn not to be afraid, to be a man, and I'd scream and wail at the images of murder, monsters and butchered bodies.

To the times when my mother shouted in the kitchen whose walls were stained with grease and damp Who wants pasta with Gruyère??? And my father would lift his hand and say Me, me, me, all of a sudden he was my age, and I'd beg her for some as well.

To the times of smells. To the times when I came home after school to the strong odor of fuel oil in the living room, because like most people in the village we heated with this cheap, blood-red fuel. The smell of fuel oil permeated our clothes, our skin, our hair.

(I'm not nostalgic for poverty, but for smells and images.)

To the times when I'd plead with my parents to let me go to the bakery to buy sweets. My father would say no, we couldn't afford it, our bill at the bakery would be too high at the end of the month, and then he'd give in, he always gave in eventually, I'd triumph, and a few minutes later I'd be in the street with the packet of multicolored sweets in my hand, a heavy plastic packet in the palm of my hand and in front of me the dirt from tractor tires.

I'm not nostalgic about poverty but about the possibility of the present.

Or rather: I hated my childhood and I miss my childhood. Is that normal?

To the times when my father used to say to me when he heard the sound of a bottle being uncorked: Someone's calling my name!

To the times when we watched TV for eight, nine hours a day because it let us think just about the present and not about tomorrow, that is our worries and our lives.

To the times when before each lottery drawing I'd look at him—always at him, the father—and feel a shiver of excitement when he said to me: Imagine we win and become millionaires.

(Of course childhood was also the times when he told me I wasn't the son he wanted, the times when the fear of running out of money defined our daily lives—but all these things touch me less and less when I think about them, I don't know why, I have no explanation.)

I'd ask him: what will we do if we become millionaires? I knew his answer, because I'd been asking him the question for years. But I pretended to be waiting to hear what he'd say. I pretended to be interested and surprised as I listened although I could have answered in his place. He'd say: First I'd buy a big TV, this big. Then I'd leave here and head for the sun.

To go back

To the days on the town square spent waiting for time to pass, or more like for time to come, talking to the women gathered at the primary school gate, trying to hear more about how the butcher's wife caught him sleeping with the woman next door.

(I know that if I went back I'd hate this world, yet I miss it.)

To the times when my biggest dream was to have a moped, like the other guys, so I could go to the McDonald's in the nearest town, twenty or so kilometers away.

To the times when I'd spend the afternoons lying on the grass beside Elena.

To the times when she'd fall asleep in the cinema with her head on my shoulder.

To the times when what made me happiest and helped me put up with the week at school was knowing that on Saturday I'd take the bus into town with my cousin Dylan and we'd spend the afternoon at the supermarket between two and six, unable to buy anything but a can of Coke or an iced tea, but happy to be there, surrounded by an infinite, unattainable abundance, by the infinite accumulation of goods we could never afford, and that we'd repeat the journey every Saturday without exception, and get the same pleasure every time.

Wealthier people went to the theater or the opera, we dreamed of the supermarket.

To the times when my mother would shrug and say What a shitty life we have.

To the times when she smiled anyway.

To the times when I could still talk to her.

To the times when I dreamed.

But I know it's too late. These impressions came back into my head the last time I thought about them—the buildings around me, the traffic farther off, the smell of food in the streets, the purple lights of Montparnasse—they came back but while I was thinking about them I already knew that it was too late. I kept walking, the sound of my footsteps on the cobblestones, and told myself that night was coming, it was time to go home and sleep.

SOURCES FOR PASSAGES
QUOTED IN THE TEXT

Jean Genet, *The Thief's Journal*, translated by Bernard Frechtman, Grove Press, 1964. Originally published as *Journal du voleur*, Gallimard, 1949.

Alice Walker, "My Father's Country Is the Poor," *The New York Times*, March 21, 1977.

Didier Eribon, *Returning to Reims*, translated by Michael Lucey, Allen Lane, 2018. Originally published as *Retour à Reims*, Librairie Arthème Fayard, 2009.

Édouard Louis, *The End of Eddy*, translated by Michael Lucey, Farrar, Straus and Giroux, 2017. Originally published as *En finir avec Eddy Belle-gueule*, Éditions du Seuil, 2014.